TOMORROW IN SHANGHAI

AND OTHER STORIES

. . .

Tomorrow in Shanghai

AND

OTHER STORIES

.....

May-lee Chai

BLAIR

Printed in the United States of America
Cover design by Laura Williams
Interior design by April Leidig

Blair is an imprint of Carolina Wren Press.

The mission of Blair/Carolina Wren Press is to seek out, nurture, and
promote literary work by new and underrepresented writers.

We gratefully acknowledge the ongoing support of general operations by the
Durham Arts Council's United Arts Fund and the North Carolina Arts Council.

These stories are works of fiction. As in all fiction, the literary perceptions and
insights are based on experience; however, all names, characters, places, and incidents
are either products of the author's imagination or are used fictitiously.
No reference to any real person is intended or should be inferred.

The following stories were previously published in slightly different forms in the
following publications: "Tomorrow in Shanghai," *Missouri Review*, Honorable Mention,
Jeffrey E. Smith Editor's Prize; "Life on Mars," *Missouri Review*, runner-up for Jeffrey E.
Smith Editor's Prize; "Hong's Mother," *Shenandoah*, nominated for a Pushcart Prize;
"White Rabbits," *Eleven Eleven*; "Jia," *Michigan Quarterly Review*.

Library of Congress Cataloging-in-Publication Data
Names: Chai, May-lee, author.
Title: Tomorrow in Shanghai : and other stories / May-lee Chai.
Other titles: Tomorrow in Shanghai (Compilation)
Description: Durham : Blair, [2022]
Identifiers: LCCN 2021060148 (print) | LCCN 2021060149 (ebook) |
ISBN 9781949467864 (paperback) | ISBN 9781949467871 (ebook)
Subjects: LCGFT: Short stories.
Classification: LCC PS3553.H2423 T66 2022 (print) | LCC PS3553.H2423 (ebook) |
DDC 813/.54—dc23/eng/20220310
LC record available at https://lccn.loc.gov/2021060148
LC ebook record available at https://lccn.loc.gov/2021060149

For my father, Winberg Chai 翟文伯

CONTENTS

TOMORROW IN SHANGHAI

AND OTHER STORIES

. . .

Tomorrow in Shanghai

· · · · ·

Zhang Xiaobing would not have considered himself a bad person, should anyone have been given the opportunity to pose such a question to the prisoner. In fact, if asked by anyone other than the court-appointed defense attorney whose main function in the trial was to enter Zhang's guilty plea, the prosecutor, and the panel of three judges who had found him guilty and sentenced him to death, very few people who knew Zhang would have said he was a bad person, wicked, evil, corrupt, a low-born thing, a turtle's egg, a nonhuman devil whose crimes would merit the ultimate punishment.

Friends and acquaintances alike might merely have said, "Young Zhang, ah? He's all right. He can get things done." Or, "If you need some business finished, Young Zhang can help you." Or even, "Heavens! That Zhang Xiaobing, he saved my son's life. Brought a doctor from the county seat all the way in that truck of his. He's really something. A real Han. Such a kind man."

But, of course, of the 274 villagers he'd helped in the nearly two decades that he'd served as a cadre in his hometown, slowly moving up the ranks since his days as a man in his early thirties just returned from a stint as a soldier in the People's Liberation Army after a career-ending leg injury, not one of his neighbors was asked what they personally thought of Assistant Village Head Zhang. And if or when any of them had offered their unprompted personal opinion of the man who was uncle, great-uncle, nephew, cousin, second cousin, third cousin once removed to almost every male surnamed Zhang in the village, the official police report did not record them. Instead, the report contained the diverse and often contradictory accounts from other villages of the crimes that had led to his arrest, detention, and sentencing.

Officially, he was a snake, a xue tou, a "blood head" who had illegally collected and sold the blood bought from the poor, illiterate peasants throughout the province, thus causing the deaths of more than thirty-seven persons (thus far) and the infection of more than a thousand (and counting) others in the myriad remote villages nestled in the mountains and plains just south of the Yellow River in the province that was once the cradle of Chinese civilization, where giant Buddhas carved into mountainsides gazed serenely heavenward, as though such crimes could not possibly occur here.

Certainly, no one asked Zhang's wife, Tang Tianyi, what she felt of the matter. She had died of a protracted and expensive illness, leaving nothing but debts behind. As for his young son, the boy had simply disappeared along with Zhang's parents, just before Zhang had been arrested some three months earlier.

The authorities suspected that the brazen criminal Zhang Xiaobing had sent them to a city on the coast, just three more people with thick provincial accents to hide amid the floating population of China's megacities. Impossible to track down, although the provincial authorities had used whatever connections they could muster—uncles or brothers in the military, other police chiefs, people who owed them favors—to keep their eyes peeled. (Naturally, their connections merely rolled their eyes at the naivete of their country cousins, all the while promising, "Sure, sure, I'll ask around. Terrible, it's terrible what this man Zhang has done." Then they promptly forgot about the three missing peasants. They had business to conduct. Life in the city. *Aiya! You had to stay on your toes. No time for village nonsense.*)

Still, having done their best, the police and county officials remained concerned about Zhang's parents and the missing son. Leaving relatives alive and guiltless could cause trouble in the future. But as stated earlier, the wizened old man with the high cheekbones, his round doughy-faced wife, and the slightly myopic but otherwise quite able twelve-year-old son of Zhang went missing and were now gone, hidden, needles in the giant haystack of urban China's migrant worker population. Like all peasants, not quite blending in and yet completely invisible to urban eyes.

"They're as good as dead! They won't dare to show up around here again."

"They'll never make it by themselves! They'll starve to death on their own!"

"Zhang's son will wash windows on Shenzhen's skyscrapers. He'll grow up pouring concrete and climbing bamboo scaffolding in Beijing, and who will remember he was ever alive?"

"And those two old heads." The county police chief used the derogatory term for the elderly, even though his own parents were as old as Zhang's. "If they don't starve selling tea eggs on the side of the road, they'll catch a cold and die in a hospital, leaving debts and nothing more for that boy." The man spat tea leaves on the carpet of the conference room of the county Public Security Bureau. He'd forgotten he wasn't at home where the floor was concrete and where he spat his tea leaves as he pleased.

Thus, Zhang Xiaobing was shot in the back of the head at 11:07 a.m. on the twenty-seventh of April, and within sixty seconds—for the timing was of the utmost importance—his still-warm corpse was dragged into the ambulance waiting at the side of the execution grounds, and a trained doctor began to extract his organs.

The local police looked at the young doctor with a mixture of suspicion and awe. He was obviously well educated and smart. They watched how he washed his hands, tied on his face mask, put on the latex gloves; he was a city boy all right. Probably born in a city, they agreed. His skin was pale, and he had those soft hands. Plus, he was wearing glasses with fashionable frames like nothing they'd seen in the county seat before. Like something on satellite TV. Like a Korean soap opera star. Yes, that's exactly what he looked like. The provincial authorities had come through in the end and pressed for a real expert to help bring this "situation" to an end.

The young doctor had taken Zhang's blood forty-eight hours before the execution to test for HIV; hepatitis A, B, and C; TB; and a host of parasites and sexually transmitted diseases. The young doctor had no illusions about what went on in the countryside these days. You could never be too sure. He'd taken on the work because his parents already owed enough money after paying for his education, and he couldn't borrow any more from them in good conscience, and he was saving up for his imminent marriage and the apartment that his fiancée—also a doctor—wanted to buy, as well as the furniture they would need. He had not wanted to borrow from his future in-laws or his friends. He'd never recover face. His youth was behind him; he understood that perfectly as he stood in the chilly wind injecting the criminal with heparin to slow the coagulation of the blood and a mild sedative—in case the man were inclined to try something crazy, leap away, fight, something that might necessitate a second bullet, which could cause more damage to the organs than merely killing the man with one shot. Such drugs made the harvest easier.

No, he was no longer truly a young man, the doctor thought with a sigh. It was time for him to take care of his parents. His mother's health was no longer good, and if she fell ill again, he would want her to have the best healthcare China could provide, which would mean more money and favors. And so, he'd taken on this extra side job that he'd heard about through the friend of a classmate from medical school. It was not an ideal job, but this was not an ideal world, and the young doctor's obligations were heavy indeed.

He had walked to the ambulance and turned his back to the prisoner so that he would not have to watch the man die. Despite himself, he had jumped when he heard the gun fire.

When the unwashed local police officers dragged the body of the criminal to the back of the ambulance, the young doctor felt momentary disgust at their crude manners, their thick uncultured accents, the black soil beneath their nails. He washed his own hands one more time in the bucket of water they brought to him before he put on the latex gloves, which he'd had to bring himself.

Thank goodness the old doctor had warned him about the conditions in these rural parts. They'd met at the provincial hospital while he waited for the county officials' car to come and pick him up. They hadn't engaged in small talk, the young doctor and the older doctor, a veteran of many of these side jobs. There were no words about the weather, the cool morning, the cerulean of the sky here far from the coastal cities, the distant clouds on the horizon and the persistent wind, which threatened to bring rain perhaps, which would slow the commute back home—and out of this forlorn provincial backwater. The younger doctor had thought this last bit to himself but did not say it aloud, although it was highly likely the older doctor might have been thinking exactly this same thing. Sometimes there was no need to state the obvious.

The older doctor spoke to him only when the county officials arrived in their new black Buick, a driver sporting white gloves in the front seat, all three of the officials riding in the back seat. *Typical bumpkins*, the young doctor thought. That's when the older doctor had said, "Better bring your own gloves. And ask for a scalpel from the hospital here, too. Plus dry ice. They won't be prepared at their end. I'd bet money on it." The young doctor had thanked his colleague, for that's how he thought of the man now, and had done as the older man advised.

The young doctor worked quickly now, removing the dead criminal's heart and liver and finally the kidneys. One of the police officers stuck his head in the back doors. "What about the eyes?" he practically spat.

"No good. You shot him in the head."

"Oh, right." The man retreated sheepishly.

Finally, after packing the organs for transportation back to the city, he began to stitch up the wound site.

Laughter stopped him.

"Hey! Do you think you're still in Shanghai?" It was the ambulance's driver, a thin-faced man from the county seat, a scrawny mustache inching above his upper lip like an underfed caterpillar. "Think you're a plastic surgeon now?"

"What about the family?" the young doctor asked, rather testily. He didn't like the crude man's mocking tone.

"They won't dare show their faces. I know these types. I've done this before, you know."

"Of course, you're right. I wasn't thinking." The young doctor cut the suture and put his needle back on the instrument tray.

"It's okay." The driver nodded sagely. "You'll get used to this." Then he handed the young doctor his pack of cigarettes. An American brand. Marlboros. Expensive.

The young doctor slipped off his gloves and threw them away in the provisional trash can beside the corpse. Then he took the cigarette and climbed down from the back of the ambulance.

While he and the driver smoked, the police officers stepped up and pulled the corpse out of the back and wrapped it quickly in a thick, black plastic bag. They carried it off to an unmarked van. The young doctor made a point of turning so that he did not have to watch anymore. He stood smoking with the driver, neither man speaking, in the clear, crisp air. The wind picked up, chilling him to the bone.

At least he's a real criminal, the young doctor thought in consolation, for he'd read the court transcripts and even compared the prisoner's face with the pictures from the file of Zhang Xiaobing's crimes. He wanted to be sure. He'd heard the horror stories of people executed for petty crimes, debts owed on land that local officials wanted to confiscate, even prostitution. The young doctor was not completely naive. And so he'd stared hard at the round-faced man in the photograph and looked carefully at the shaven-headed man he'd taken blood from two days ago.

Zhang had lost weight during his time in prison, but he was still recognizable from his former days as an assistant village head with graying hair and a too-loud sports jacket over his unfashionable polyester shirt. They hadn't spoken. Zhang hadn't tried to engage the young doctor in even the most innocuous and inane conversation. *Have you eaten yet? A long ride from the city?* Or worse, *Can you deliver a message to my family?* None of the nightmare questions the young doctor had imagined a manipulative and desperate criminal might ask. Instead the man before him had stared straight ahead, his eyes glazed, an interior gaze. Perhaps the man felt guilty about his crimes, or maybe he was merely sorry that he'd been caught. The young doctor consoled himself with this thought.

The prisoner knows he's done wrong.

The prisoner won't try to resist.

Maybe some good will come of this man's life after all, he thought, meaning the organs, of course. They were in good shape. Valuable. They'd bring a good price for the hospital.

He did not allow himself to think, *How does a bumpkin like this even get a job buying blood for a county hospital? Did he receive any training? Even if he'd suspected the job was illegal, could such a man have afforded to turn it down?*

There was no point in thinking too much. Only trouble could come from such thoughts.

In this brave new world, all jobs required some unexpected risk.

Certainly, the young man hadn't foreseen interacting with prisoners in seedy rural backwaters in his future when he'd been accepted into medical school. No, he'd been naive and hopeful in those days.

Without so much as glancing over his shoulder to watch the un-marked van drive the corpse away, the doctor rapped on the door of the county officials' Buick waiting to take him back to the city. The locks clicked open. He threw his cigarette into the weeds on the side of the dirt road and climbed inside.

. . .

On his ride back to the provincial hospital, the coolers with the or-gans arrayed on the seat beside him, the young doctor did not notice the lushness of the sorghum fields that lay just beyond the edges of the new and nearly deserted highway. In the distance, running paral-lel to the multilane highway, was a slightly elevated dirt road where an old man was driving a wooden cart pulled by an ox. A younger man buzzed past him on a motorbike and the ox snorted once, pulling his head back. The old man called out, and the ox steadied itself and continued on its way, as stolid as if it were pulling a plow through a paddy.

Instead the young doctor stared only at the back of the seat in front of him as though that might speed his return to civilization. He felt slightly nauseated. The highway was brand new but already pocked and bumpy. A shoddy construction job. Every time the car shook, his left hand shot out involuntarily to steady the coolers, and every time he retracted his hand quickly.

Then the rain started, all at once, a downpour so thick the water ran across the highway like a river suddenly changed course.

"Ta ma de," the driver swore. "They built this highway lower than all the roads around here. We're in a valley! Think about it! When it rains, everything drains onto the pavement. Stupid turtle eggs."

"Will we be able to make it back in time?" the young doctor asked nervously.

"Oh, sure. I've driven in worse weather than this. It's just a pain."

"Good. I mean, it's good you have experience."

"It's my job." The driver shrugged. "I'm no surgeon like you, but I can drive in a rainstorm."

"Well, you have one skill I don't."

The driver laughed good-naturedly.

Then there was nothing more to say, and they fell back into the same uncomfortable silence.

I'll feel better when I'm home. Out of the boondocks. The young doctor tried to console himself. He'd definitely feel better tomorrow in Shanghai.

Life on Mars

· · · · ·

In the morning, there were jade-colored fields of corn stretching as far as the eye could see. The three-hour drive from Denver had been dark; Guo Yu hadn't seen anything but the black road and the taillights of the cars and trucks around Uncle's car. From the window of his new bedroom, however, he could see for miles, all the way to the horizon, the emptiness of the sky like an inverted rice bowl over the endless green fields.

It was both exactly like and nothing like the America of the movies he'd seen.

His aunt was not living with his uncle anymore. That would have surprised his parents. Yu didn't say anything when his uncle explained in the kitchen that morning, "She's with her sister," as though that explained everything. His uncle handed him a small box of dry cereal, which Yu ate straight from the box. It had a picture of a cartoon tiger on the box and too much sugar. But Yu didn't complain. He was hungry, and his parents had said not to make a fuss. He was lucky to be in America. He must do well in school, they'd said, obey Uncle and Auntie, get accepted into an American college in two years. They had not said it, but he feared that they also expected him at that point to find an American girl to marry. Then when they could, they would join him. Until then, he had to find a way to adapt. They were counting on him.

· · ·

"Hey, kid, you just gonna sit there?" His uncle's boss stood in front of Yu. Unlike his uncle, this man wore polished leather shoes that peeked out from under the cuffs of his pleated pants. He wore a clean white shirt with no stains and a complicated watch. He had a fat belly that hung over his belt. He'd been in America for a long time. Out of politeness Yu didn't stare at the man's face. He stared at the watch instead.

"No, Uncle," he said politely even though this man was not his real uncle. His real uncle stood in silence at the stove next to a large Mexican man with tattoos of dragons on his biceps. "I can work, too."

"Work?" The Boss laughed. The men in the kitchen laughed. Yu couldn't tell if his uncle was laughing with them. His eyes were on the Boss's watch. It had three faces and six second hands. Yu had seen watches like this online. One that he'd liked remained waterproof even at the bottom of the sea.

The Boss put his hand on top of Yu's head. He could feel the dampness of the man's sweaty palm on his scalp. "And what can you do, Little Emperor?"

Yu cringed at the nickname, but what could he say?

"I can do anything." He tried to think of something he could do. He'd been a student his entire life. He'd never worked. It was his parents' wish that he continue to study. He'd done his best at school, but his best wasn't as good as the students whose parents could afford private schools and private tutors. His teachers had liked him. He was a personable boy with a pleasant personality, but he lacked genius or, barring genius, the work ethic needed to make up for his family's lack of resources.

"I can sweep the floor," he said, thinking of things he'd seen workers doing. "I can wash the dishes."

"Whoa, whoa, listen to this! The Little Emperor really does want to work!" The Boss laughed. He pulled a pack of cigarettes out of the pocket of his crisp white shirt and tapped one out for himself. "Fine,

fine, glad to hear you can be useful," he said. "A kid who's willing to work." He tapped the Mexican man between the shoulder blades. "Roberto," he said in English, "show the kid where the mop is."

Yu's heart jumped inside his ribcage. He suddenly wondered if the man would pay him directly—to earn real American dollars. He wouldn't tell his parents; they'd be worried, they'd want him to study, but he could imagine how money of his own might be useful.

So Yu learned to mop floors and wash the windows and keep busy and useful.

■ ■ ■

That evening, they were closing up. It had been fourteen hours. There weren't many customers. The restaurant was located off the exit of the highway before anyone entered the actual town, so occasionally some truckers and campers and tourists stopped by. They pulled into the gas station next door, then wandered over to the restaurant. They ordered some of the strange items on the menu that Yu had never heard of before: fried rice with pineapple and a pink sweet sauce that smelled as bad as it tasted, gummy fried noodles with three kinds of tough meats, scrambled eggs with a thick brown gravy poured on top.

After lunch but before dinner, around 3:30 in the afternoon, the Boss allowed his employees to eat, so Yu sat with his uncle in the corner booth while the pretty young waitress sat with the Mexican man at another table.

"What kind of food is this?" Yu asked.

His uncle shrugged. "The Americans like it."

Yu looked at the empty restaurant, the empty parking lot. "How do you know?" The few tourists who'd come in had left their plates half full.

Uncle shook his head. "Don't ask questions here. This is the way it is."

Yu knew that his aunt and uncle had given the Boss's family in China a lot of money so that he would sponsor them for a green card. They'd borrowed the money from a lot of people. That kind of money took a long time to pay off.

• • •

That night his uncle slept the sleep of the dead. Yu could hear him snoring in the bedroom across the hall.

Yu couldn't sleep. He wondered how his parents were doing. He wondered if they knew what they'd gotten him into. But he couldn't disappoint them. He knew they'd borrowed a lot of money to send him to America. They'd paid brokers who'd helped get Yu the right kind of visa, who'd coached him through his interview with the American visa officer, who'd greased the right palms so he'd obtained his passport in a timely manner. They'd paid money to Uncle and Auntie to take care of him.

He wondered if his aunt had taken the money and that's why her husband was stuck working in this restaurant by himself. He wondered if his uncle was angry.

• • •

The next day, Yu worked all day again. By evening, his back hurt from the mopping. There'd been a spill in the dining room, the floor was sticky with Coca-Cola and the sweet red sauce from the dishes.

He was dumping the mop water on the edge of the parking lot, mainly to escape the heat of the kitchen, where the cook was watching the TV in the corner. The station was entirely in Spanish, and Yu hadn't understood a word. He'd worried that his English wouldn't be good enough in America, but he hadn't had to speak English at all in the days since his arrival.

He stood at the edge of the parking lot, staring up at the stars glittering in the black sky. Most nights at home it was too polluted to see the stars, but every night the sky was clear here, the stars enormous, bright.

He hadn't noticed the boys approaching.

A *ping!* like a shot from an air rifle ricocheted off the dumpster's metal side. He spun around immediately. There was a group of boys on bicycles, fancy bikes, the kind he'd seen on TV, the kind you could do tricks with: wide tires, low handlebars, bright colors. Expensive.

"What're you doing here?" A boy with a round face and flat nose pointed his chin at Yu. He had extremely close-set eyes and a very broad forehead, making his face seem more like a space alien's than a normal human's.

There was a tall boy in the back. "What's up? You speak English?"

"Hello, yes, I can speak English." Yu heard his own thin voice, too loud in his own ears.

The other two boys were thinner, acne dotting their cheeks. As they approached, Yu could see they chewed their lips. They were cowards. They would be the ones he should attack first if it came to that. It was going to come to that. He felt the hair on his neck rise. He could feel the sweat pouring from his armpits.

"Heh-roh! I speakee Engrish!" the tall boy said, and the cowardly boys laughed obediently. It was a stupid joke. Yu didn't have to understand it to know that it was dumb.

"I work for the restaurant. I am visiting—"

The boys charged, but Yu was faster than they anticipated. He grabbed one of skinny boys from behind, twisting his arms up into the air behind his back, then swung the boy around in front of him, a human shield. The alien-face boy was swinging, ready to punch; he couldn't recalibrate and ended up punching the skinny boy in the stomach.

"You idiot!" the tall boy said.

The skinny boy let out a grunt and slumped in Yu's arms. Then he threw up onto the hot asphalt.

"Sick," the alien-face boy exclaimed.

That broke the mood.

A car pulled into the parking lot, the headlights slicing the darkness.

"Let's go!" The other boys hopped onto their bicycles and rode away into the night, leaving their injured friend behind.

The kitchen door opened, and Yu could see a man silhouetted, the golden light pouring around him from behind. For a second, he was worried it was the Boss or his uncle and he would get in trouble. But the man was shorter, stocky, the cook. And Yu knew he'd be okay.

He left the skinny boy to lie on the asphalt, catching his breath, or vomiting again, something, and Yu went back inside.

• • •

Yu struggled with what to tell his parents. He'd promised to write them a letter every week, but words to describe his new situation escaped him. They would not want to hear about the boys. They would admonish him only, telling him not to get in trouble, certainly not to fight. He didn't want to tell them about his missing aunt either. He was afraid his mother would be alarmed, might even insist that he come back home. He certainly did not know how to describe his own feelings of bewilderment, this pressure in his chest and dry lump in his throat that blocked all the English he'd studied from coming out. Instead Yu described his uncle and aunt's home, an American house Uncle rented from the Boss with two bedrooms and a separate kitchen with a large refrigerator/freezer and its own grassy yard.

He did not tell them that the rooms were unfurnished except for the mattresses and a wooden kitchen table with four chairs that did not match. On the one day he did not work, his uncle liked to watch the television propped on the kitchen counter, but Yu did not like the shows his uncle favored—American game shows where contestants vied for prizes or else a channel that showed nothing but the news. He wanted to watch soccer, but there were no matches on any of the channels.

After writing the letter, Yu decided it was not quite right and ripped it up.

■ ■ ■

Another week passed, and the boys on the bicycles did not come back.

■ ■ ■

One day the cook brought a teenage boy to the restaurant; he was slender and tan and taller than his father.

He brought the boy up to Yu, who was sitting in a back booth rolling silverware into paper napkins for dinner.

"You can teach my son," the man said, pointing to the boy and back at Yu in an exaggerated manner. "Teach. Him." The man pantomimed writing. Clearly, the cook's exaggerated motions suggested he did not trust Yu's English to be sufficient to understand him although the man himself spoke English with a heavy accent. Yu was vaguely offended, but he was still too slow in speaking to think of a witty response.

"I need a math tutor," the boy said. "I'm in summer school."

"Okay," said Yu, even though math was his worst subject, so boring he'd stopped paying attention to his teachers long ago. Hence his parents' despair, knowing there was no way he'd ever pass the gaokao and get into any kind of university in China. They'd saved and borrowed to send him to his aunt in America. He'd start at the local high school in the fall. He knew they expected him to do well here. He wasn't sure how this was miraculously supposed to happen. "Study," his father had told him on the phone when he'd called from the airport in Denver to let them know he'd arrived safely and had met up with his uncle. "No more excuses," his father added.

(In fact, Yu was already thinking if school didn't work out, perhaps he'd go into business like his uncle and aunt, but he wasn't sure what kind of business.)

But in a turn of luck, Yu became Andrew's tutor.

At first Andrew just showed him the worksheets he was required to do as homework. Yu realized that he lacked the vocabulary in English to explain anything. He looked at the worksheets and discovered with delight that they were not complicated, not even Gao Yi–level math, the last year he'd finished in senior high, but rather the trigonometry from junior high he'd finished years earlier.

Yu took over Andrew's pencil and completed the sheets rapidly without speaking.

Fortunately, Andrew did not complain. He said, "Cool. Thanks. Do you want to play Super Mario?"

They walked from the restaurant to Andrew's house on the other side of town. Yu had not seen much of the town yet. His uncle was always working or sleeping or watching television. He'd driven Yu to the Safeway grocery store, and Yu had been disappointed by the unfamiliar offerings.

Fortunately, they mostly ate at the restaurant, so Yu hadn't had to worry about adjusting to American food besides the dishes they served there.

Now they passed a taxidermy shop with antlers above the door and heads of dead animals in the large window, a shop selling what appeared to be things other people had thrown away, a Dairy Queen, houses, then the small downtown with its squat brick buildings, bars, a pizzeria, more bars, then they were walking across a bridge over railroad tracks. Finally they arrived in a neighborhood of small houses huddled close to each other.

In the fifth house from the corner, a house with no distinguishing features, not even a tree or plants in the front yard, they played Nintendo sitting on the floor side by side until it was dark, and Yu, noticing, said, "I should go back. I have to work."

Andrew said, "It's never busy this time of year. Not until the college kids get back. They're all rich and eat out all the time."

But Yu called the restaurant just in case. Uncle spoke briefly on the phone. He was in the kitchen; Yu could hear the sizzle of the wok in the background, the unmistakable hiss of steam from the boiling soup pots. He could almost feel the humidity on his skin. He was glad not to be in the restaurant. It was better with Andrew in the house. Although it was small and cramped and dark, it smelled clean, like lemons and something else Yu couldn't identify yet.

"I spoke to Roberto," Uncle said. "If his son gets an A, he will pay you. Make sure he gets an A."

"It's easy. Kid math," Yu said.

"Don't make any mistakes," his uncle said and hung up.

"Was that Chinese, dude?" Andrew asked. "Cool, you gotta teach me some Chinese!"

And Andrew made some noises like a character fighting in a movie and waving his hands in the air like Jet Li, but Yu forgave him.

■ ■ ■

Andrew had long dark lashes framing his large brown eyes. He had a slight scar on the right side of his jaw. He had fleshy earlobes and a tattoo of a small star on the side of his neck.

"Your parents let you do this?" Yu pointed at the star.

"No, not really. A friend did that for me."

"Did it hurt?"

"Yeah, so I'm going to wait till I'm older and can get a real one. I want an X-wing here," he flexed his long tan arm, the bicep bulging, "and a Darth Vader here," he pointed to his hairy right calf. "You got any tatts?"

Tatts, thought Yu, tucking the word away into his memory. "Not yet," he said.

■ ■ ■

Andrew got an A on his worksheets. There were a few errors, problems marked with a red X that Yu hadn't remembered how to work or else hadn't double-checked and had made errors, but that only made Andrew's progress seem more realistic in the teacher's eyes. "Good job!" she wrote on the top in red, drawing a smiley face next to the A. Yu could not imagine one of his teachers in China ever doing such a thing. Andrew's father was pleased although he did not immediately offer Yu any money. Perhaps, Yu figured, he was waiting for the final grade at the end of the summer. Uncle was pleased and allowed Yu to spend more time tutoring Andrew in the afternoons when Andrew came back from his morning classes. That meant hours and hours away from the restaurant and a kind of freedom that Yu had never experienced before.

They borrowed bikes from a neighbor and cycled around the small town, through its main park that featured a few picnic tables and a rudimentary swing set for small children. They rode through the campus of the university, with its large stone buildings and strange abstract sculptures. One afternoon they biked to a river. Andrew said they could go swimming.

Yu didn't have a suit. Andrew said it didn't matter. He stripped to his underpants and jumped in. Yu followed him.

The water was freezing. Yu felt his testicles retreat into his body, the hairs on his limbs stand on end.

"Come on! Beat you to the other side!" Andrew dove into the wave, splashing and kicking, and swam away.

Yu did not know how to swim. It was ironic given that his name was a homonym for fish, but where would he have ever had the place to learn? His high school had had no swimming pool, and sports training was not wasted on ordinary students without exceptional ability.

Still, Yu felt he understood the principle.

He watched Andrew swimming away, and he tried to wade after him until the tug of the current was too strong and the rocks beneath his feet too sharp and he slipped into the water. He tried to paddle, pumping his arms, and for a while this worked and he was able to keep his head above the water. Then the current grabbed him, and he was hurtling down the river, farther and farther from the sun-drenched spot on the shore where Andrew was scrambling through the reeds and onto the bank.

Yu tried to lengthen his body, imagining that if he could stretch onto his back, he could float, and he almost remembered a time when as a small child his Ye Ye had taken him to a pool at a local university, had paid for lessons. He'd developed an earache, and his mother had stopped the lessons before he'd learned to do more than float on his back. His grandfather had died not long after, and his parents had never bothered to take him back to the pool.

Yu did not want to die like this. Panic made his heart beat even faster than the exertion, and he flailed his arms and pumped his legs and held his head above the cold water and then he swirled into something hard. A tree limb. A root. Something growing in the river, and he grabbed hold. He clung to the tree with both arms and eventually caught his breath. Then he put his legs down and realized this part of the river was quite shallow. He could walk to the shore.

He pulled himself up onto the bank, the water heavy against his frozen limbs, and then fell heavily onto the dirt. He was shaking. He lay on the ground in the sun and could not control the motion of his limbs.

Andrew came running along the bank. He was shouting Yu's name. It sounded like, "You, you! Hey, you!" Then Andrew was kneeling beside Yu's body, rubbing his hands up and down Yu's legs, his arms, slapping his chest. "You! Are you okay, You?"

Andrew stretched on the dirt beside Yu, rubbing Yu's chest with both arms, holding Yu's back against his chest, warming him with his own body.

Gradually, Yu stopped shaking from the cold.

. . .

They walked back the quarter mile Yu had drifted down the river, back to the spot opposite where they'd left their bikes. Andrew swam back across and grabbed their clothes and climbed on his bike and rode around to the bridge higher up the river and came back for Yu. Yu put his jeans and T-shirt back on.

"I didn't know you didn't know how to swim," Andrew said.

"I don't know how to swim *in a river*," Yu said, with dignity.

They didn't speak for the rest of their ride back to Andrew's house. Yu didn't go to work in the restaurant that night. Instead he walked home to the house he shared with Uncle. He wanted to be alone to process his feelings, the memory of the day. He didn't want it soiled with the men's crude talk in the kitchen or the smell of grease or the whininess of the customers.

. . .

That night when Uncle came home, he said he'd heard about the swimming accident from Roberto. Andrew had apparently called his father to apologize, fearing Yu would get in trouble for missing work. The Boss understood, too, and said Yu didn't need to come into work tomorrow. He should rest, recover.

Roberto apologized to Uncle then and said he hadn't realized his son would put his nephew in danger. He said his son would have to study on his own. Yu didn't need to tutor him. It was time his son learned to take responsibility as a man and to stop playing around.

"No!" Yu almost shouted. "I have to keep tutoring him. There's three weeks to the final." His mind was racing. He hadn't imagined such a terrible consequence to such a wonderful day. "Besides," he added, thinking quickly, "I haven't been paid."

"Don't worry," his uncle said. "I'll make him pay you for your work."

"No," Yu said. "I have to continue. If he gets an A in the class, they'll pay me more. Andrew told me. If I stop now, he won't get the A. Believe me. I know."

"You were supposed to be studying at his house. Why were you at the river?"

"He can't study that long. He's not used to it. He needed to take a break."

His uncle looked unconvinced. "He's a wild boy. Be careful."

"You have to tell his father that I have to keep tutoring him. It's better than working in the restaurant. If he does well, I can tutor other kids when school starts. I need the money. My parents can't afford to send me anything more. They spent everything just to get me here."

His uncle considered this. "You're right," he said at last. Money trumped everything. They both understood that about their lives. "I'll speak to his father tomorrow."

After that, Uncle sat down in front of the television as he did every night. He took out his pack of Marlboros and watched the news, blowing blue smoke from his nostrils. The smoke hung around his head like clouds.

The American president was on the news. He said he was sending a spaceship to Mars to look for signs of life, and Uncle exploded with anger. "He's going to get us all killed!" He continued to rant at the television.

Yu didn't try to argue with his uncle. He watched the newscaster sitting before a graphic of ice then black space then a large red planet that must have been Mars. Yu didn't know if it was really the planet or a special effect. He closed his eyes and tried to imagine traveling through space, but against the red-black screen of his eyelids, all that came to him was the feeling of his body hurtling down the river. He opened his eyes quickly.

. . .

The next day Andrew called from the restaurant. "My dad says I can keep studying with you." He hung up then without saying anything more.

Yu understood his reticence to speak in front of the other men. They could spoil everything.

That night Yu lay in his bed remembering the feel of Andrew's body against his, the warmth of his skin, the hammering of his heart against his ribs. Was it Andrew's heartbeat or his own?

■ ■ ■

That weekend Yu's parents called. They were worried that he hadn't written, but they expressed this as anger. "We are wasting money on this call!" his mother said. "Your father and I have to work every day just to pay for you to stay in America, and all you can do is make us waste more money!"

Yu apologized. "I'm working. I am a summer school tutor."

"Teaching what?" his parents wanted to know.

When he told them math, they both laughed.

"Don't try to fool us," his father said.

"How is Auntie?" his mother asked.

"Busy, working all the time." Yu figured that he was not lying. Wherever she was, what else would she be doing?

"You promised to write every week," his mother said. Her voice broke at the other end of the line. "I think about you every day. Do you think about us? Have you forgotten your mother? I worry about you all the time."

"I'm sorry. I'll write to you," he promised.

Then they hung up. International calls were expensive.

■ ■ ■

That evening, Yu wrote a letter to his parents as he sat on the floor of his bedroom.

Dear Ba, Ma,
How are you? I am doing fine. I am working hard every day. I
obey Uncle and study and work. I am making a friend. Don't
worry. I think of you every day.

He stopped. How to describe America? Nothing came to him that
would help his parents to understand the scent of grass on the wind,
the bright stars in the night sky, the empty sidewalks, the space everywhere, the boring restaurant, the boring news, swimming with
Andrew.

He thought of something and continued:

U.S. President Clinton spoke on TV. He said the U.S. will
send a spaceship to collect data from Mars. It will not land
until 1997, on July 4, the American Independence Day. What
do you think about life on Mars? Can you believe it?

Uncle says that Americans should not go to Mars. He says
if there is life there, it will not be friendly. We should not trouble
it. We should not let it know that we exist until we are very
strong and can travel in space all the time and can protect
ourselves from the aliens.

Personally, I am not afraid. If the Martians are so power-
ful, then why have they not already attacked us? And if they
are weak, perhaps they will be afraid of us. I can see the stars
and the planets at night from my bedroom window. The sky is
very clear here. I can see Mars at night. Perhaps there is a boy
on Mars looking out his window at Earth in the sky. Or maybe
he is already dead. Or maybe he will be born someday in the
future when I am already gone.

Uncle is afraid of Mars but I am your son and I am not
afraid.

Life on Mars must be very interesting, I think.

Satisfied with his letter, Yu signed his name with a flourish and folded the paper into squares and then triangles until the whole letter was the shape of a fish. This was a trick he'd learned at school. He thought his parents would appreciate the symbolism, the wish for abundance for them and a reminder of him.

He laid the letter on the floor next to the mattress, then lay back on the pillow so that he could still see out the window, watch the moon trek across the dark sky, knowing on the other side of the earth, the sun was rising, his parents were getting up for work, they were thinking of him.

Yu decided that he would tell Andrew that he knew now what he wanted his tatt to be. A small red circle on his ankle. Mars, he'd say. Beside it, a single blue line. A river. He'd let Andrew make the cuts, insert the ink. It would be there always, a reminder that life was possible even on this strange alien world.

The Monkey King of Sichuan

. . . . .

"What is it?" Esther sat up in her chair. The last time one of Esther's friends had refused to tell her something over the phone, it turned out that the woman had been raped. She was so traumatized, so ashamed that she could not voice the words except face-to-face. Esther hoped that wasn't the case this time.

"I'll tell you when I see you Saturday." Esther could hear Grace inhale deeply. "I don't want to say now."

"Okay. Are you all right?"

"Oh, yes. I'm fine. It will be good to see you!"

. . .

Saturday afternoon, Esther drove to Palo Alto, but she realized only too late that she should have left San Francisco earlier. There was unexpected traffic on 101, then more on El Camino. She'd agreed to meet Grace at 3:30, and it was already twenty after. Finally the exit for Palm Drive came up. Esther ran the yellow light as it turned to red.

Esther spotted a couple getting their wedding pictures taken amidst the tall, orderly arrangement of palm trees. It was a beautiful late November day, the yellow sunlight bright, the sky blue, no cloud in sight. Picture perfect. When she'd first moved to San Francisco, Esther was surprised by all her coworkers' wedding photos taken on the Stanford campus. She had assumed they were alumni and was moved that they'd all chosen to work for a nonprofit. Then she'd realized, no, it was just a popular place for wedding photos, perhaps even more popular with people with no connection to the school.

Luck shone on Esther, and she found a parking place. She got out quickly and walked rapidly up the broad sidewalk toward the beige sandstone colonnades of the campus. She glanced at her watch. 3:27 p.m.

As she passed the shrubs lining the way to the Cantor Center, Esther was shocked to come across the bride and groom again, this time in front of her. Then she realized it was a different couple. The first couple had been a white man with an Asian woman, but this couple were both Asians.

"Hold it!" a man's voice shouted, and Esther jumped, looking around, before she realized it was the photographer.

The Asian bride and groom were standing face-to-face, the colonnades in the background, a giant metallic scrim angled above them on a black pole while the photographer's assistant fluffed the bride's train.

"Hold it! That's great! Now smile!" the photographer commanded, followed by the metallic sound of the electronic flash firing.

"Don't touch it," the bride snapped.

"But there's something—" the groom said.

"Hold it!" Another flash.

"Honey. Don't. Touch. My. Veil," the bride snarled through her frozen smile.

Esther didn't want to ruin their shot, but she also didn't want to have to wait till these people were done with their photo session.

She made a dash for the Cantor Center. "Excuse me, sorry, excuse me!" she called behind her.

Everything about the center was imposing, the widely spaced white columns, the tiny steps, everything meant to mimic architecture from an ancient temple. Nothing like the state university where Esther and Grace had done their graduate studies. Esther couldn't recall now what any particular building looked like, but at least the landscaping had been nice, flowers in season, a creek with a turtle pond. She remembered walking from one classroom building to the next and looking up at the blue sky and the mountains in the horizon and being captivated by the beauty. She had never felt intimidated by the architecture, though there were other things there that had been intimidating.

Grace was waiting outside the coat check.

"Sorry, I'm late! Were you waiting long?" Esther waved to Grace. "You look fantastic!" Grace was wearing an elegantly tailored navy suit jacket over an abstract print silk shift. No one dressed up at the nonprofit where Esther worked. She hadn't bothered to upgrade her wardrobe much since grad school, where they'd all favored casual, cheap clothing.

Grace grabbed Esther's shoulders and hugged her warmly. Esther hadn't grown up hugging people, so it always felt a little weird, and Grace certainly hadn't hugged people in China, but maybe this was popular among the teachers at the boarding school where Grace was teaching now. "It's so good to see you, Esther!" She handed Esther a map. "They gave this to me when I put my bag in the coat check."

"Thanks." Esther glanced at the map. "So what is the school like? Do you like Massachusetts?"

"It's pretty," Grace said. "My school is very rural. Lots of trees. And really devoted to physical education. It's our motto: 'Strong mind, strong character, strong body.'"

"Ugh, how fascist."

"I have to learn how to ride a horse. Can you believe it? Me! We all have to take turns leading activities, and my service was deferred for two years. But now my time is up!" Grace laughed. "I told them I don't know how, but they said they will pay someone to teach me."

"Maybe you can get a doctor to write a letter, say it's bad for your back or something?"

They passed through the atrium, another imposing space, with a vaulted ceiling, the second floor tiered by more white columns, two marble staircases, and even the floor itself a work of art, a beautifully patterned mosaic. "Look at this place," Esther whistled.

They passed by a glass case containing a metal and clay breakfast setting complete with eggs, toast, coffee, a bowl of oatmeal.

"What is this supposed to be?" Grace wrinkled her nose.

"Little Leland's Last Breakfast, David Gilhooly," Esther read from the placard. "Ha! Somebody has a sense of humor. Do you know the origin story? Stanford had this university built as a memorial after his young son died."

"*Morbid* humor," said Grace.

"I'd rather see a monument to the Chinese railroad workers whose wages he stole."

"Even more morbid!"

They toured the first exhibit in silence. The Cantor Center held a lot of contemporary abstract art in its permanent collection. Grace stood before a large canvas exploring the textures of white paint. "I don't understand this," she said, shaking her head.

"Let's try upstairs."

"At least the building is very beautiful," Grace said, admiring the view of the atrium.

"More white columns," Esther said.

The upstairs gallery had a special exhibition titled "Fame/Unfame" with works exploring "the duality of fame, the public's gaze, and the fleeting nature of adoration," according to a sign on the wall of the first gallery.

"Hmph," Esther said.

"Did you hear Ha Jin just won the National Book Award?" Grace asked.

"Yes of course." Esther squinted at the first in a series of Diane Arbus photographs. She'd always felt Arbus's photos were a little mean, but she couldn't deny that they were powerful. She stared at the black-and-white portrait of twin sisters, standing shoulders squared before the camera. "I can see what inspired Stanley Kubrick."

"Which do you think is more important? The Pulitzer Prize or the National Book Award?" asked Grace. "As a Chinese, I don't know what's the difference."

"Hmm. That's a good question." Esther considered the prizes but realized she had no idea how such awards were determined. "The Pulitzer is more famous, I think. Most people in America have heard of it." They moved into a room of hyper-realistic paintings of people and objects from their suburban homes. "I don't know if most people think about the National Book Award per se. But book people know." Esther stared at one large canvas of white people sitting on chaise lounges before a pool. "Are these people famous, or are they just rich?" She squinted at the placard.

"I notice Americans like stories about the Cultural Revolution," Grace said. "Professor Brooks told me I should write my dissertation on literature about the Cultural Revolution so that it will be published."

"God, he was always so bossy," Esther said. Brooks was considered a bigwig in the department, well known in the literary world, used to getting his way. She felt humiliated by the way he'd marked up her papers in red ink (like he'd cut a vein while grading, she used to complain), even making suggestions on her syntax, word choice, well beyond what other professors would comment on. "What did you originally want to write about?"

"I didn't have any idea. That's why I asked him."

"Oh, they have Warhol's Mao prints!" Esther remarked as they turned the corner.

"You see," Grace said, nodding.

They stood before a wall arrayed with the colorful silk-screen prints: Mao with a blue face and green lips, Mao with an orange face and red lips, red-face Mao with white lips. Grace took a step back to the center of the room, took out her camera from her purse, and snapped a picture.

"Warhol was a genius," Grace said at last. "I think he is the only Western artist who understood about Mao."

They moved into the next room, and there was a black-and-white charcoal drawing of a nude woman, her legs splayed. "Untitled (Reclining Female Nude), nineteen seventy-four," Esther read aloud. "I wonder if this is supposed to represent fame or unfame?"

"I think American women are very strong," Grace said. "They have many rights."

Esther looked at the drawing again. It didn't necessarily convey strength as she'd define it. But Grace wasn't looking at the picture. She was staring out the window at the end of the gallery, at the treetops visible against the clear sky, the Stanford clock tower in the distance. "What do you mean?"

"Like the professor who sued the department," Grace said. "Only an American woman can do that."

The professor was the most recent hire in the unfortunately named Oriental Studies Department at their alma mater. The name was a sore point with students, but as the dean had explained, it was a "heritage name," dating from an era with different sensibilities. The department was well known across the U.S. for the scholarship and productivity of its faculty—one of the top ten in the country; top five by some rubrics. Even the lawsuit, which was settled out of court, had done little to dent the department's reputation.

"A Chinese woman could never do what she did," Grace said. "Call what she did sexual harassment."

"She slept with the chair. That was her choice," Esther said. "But the chair shouldn't have retaliated against her after she broke it off. That was gross. I'm glad she sued. But she didn't really gain anything. Her career is ruined." There had been some kind of secret settlement.

Esther remembered reading about it in a newspaper account, but given that the woman was working as an adjunct at another school, it didn't seem like it could have been a lot of money, not life-changing won-the-Lotto-now-you-can-retire money. "Do you want to look at another exhibit? Or head out? We could get something to eat here in Palo Alto, or would you rather wait to eat in the city?" Esther drifted toward the exit.

"I was sexually harassed," Grace said.

Esther stopped in her tracks.

"What? The chair harassed you after he got sued?" Esther was genuinely shocked. "What is wrong with him? Good god."

"No, it was Professor Brooks." Grace's lips were pressed tightly together. She looked stricken. Esther touched her arm.

"Brooks?"

"I slept with him," Grace said. She turned away from the window. "I wouldn't mind going. I don't really like this kind of modern art."

They walked together out of the exhibit. One end of the hallway seemed dimmer. Esther stopped and consulted the map. "This way," she said. They walked through a room of large, colorful boards of wood cut into shapes: triangles, a parallelogram, a trapezoid.

Esther's mind raced, sifting through memories. She'd left the program before Grace, before all the scandals hit. Esther's widowed father had fallen ill, and she'd had to take a leave of absence to care for him. Then it wasn't worth it coming back to grad school after being out for two years. She found a job at a nonprofit, then just drifted out of academia and into working life. But even before she left, she'd suspected that Grace had had an affair with Brooks. She'd observed the way Grace would talk to him, the softness in her voice. At the last student-faculty party that Esther had attended, Grace had offered Brooks a slice of chocolate cake from the communal table, choosing it from all the messy potluck items arrayed in a row, carrying it to him with such tender solicitousness. Esther had observed the brusque way Brooks had refused, gruffly, turning his head, embarrassed, his cheeks flushing. The look had surprised Esther at the time. Now she realized her error. He hadn't been embarrassed or ashamed, but furious. He'd slept with a student, slept with Grace, and was angry that she wasn't acting discreetly. Esther hadn't realized that Grace considered the relationship to be sexual harassment.

"Did you report him?" Esther asked.

"No, I cannot."

"Why not?"

"Brooks is a very tall tree in our field."

"You should report him."

"When I applied to my job, I asked him to write me a letter of recommendation. After I was hired, my chair said, 'Grace, your English is excellent! I'm so surprised!' Then she showed me Brooks's letter. He told them my English was not very good, that I had a very 'thick accent.' He said I couldn't write very well in English."

"Screw him! You should definitely report him!" Esther could feel her heart racing. If Grace hadn't been hired at her current school, she could have been deported. It was hard to find employers willing to sponsor someone for a green card. "You don't need him anymore. You've got other references." But Esther heard the weakness of her suggestions the moment the words left her mouth. What good would it do Grace now?

They turned once and they were back at the atrium. "Here we are," Esther said. They walked down the stairs, and Grace picked up her suitcase from the coat check.

"There must be some kind of handicap exit," Esther said. "You don't want to have to drag that down the front stairs."

A guard pointed them to an elevator, and they took it to the ground floor. They found the exit to the sculpture garden.

"Look," Esther pointed at the massive bronze nudes before them. "We're literally at the Gates of Hell."

"Ha." Grace scrutinized a placard. "Oh, Rodin. I've heard of him."

"Think of the money," Esther said. "Can you imagine going to school at a place that has actual Rodins? And nobody's even here gawking at them."

They headed toward the parking lot. The sun was setting, long shadows stretched across the sidewalk. The wind had picked up. Esther zipped up her polar fleece jacket. "Are you cold? Did you bring another jacket?"

"I'm fine! We've already had two big snows in Western Mass. This feels warm to me."

Esther noted that the brides and grooms were all gone. Two young women whizzed by on bicycles. They were perfect looking, their long brown hair pulled back in ponytails, their tan legs muscled but slim. Esther figured they had to be students here.

"Where did you want to eat? It's your trip, you decide. Do you want Chinese food? There's great dim sum. I know a Hakka place. Something else?"

"I read about a new ramen place in Japantown," Grace said. "Is that a problem?"

"Oh, that sounds great! And there's parking at the mall too."

They climbed in Esther's Honda, and she headed down Palm Drive toward El Camino Real.

"It feels good to sit down," Grace said. She pulled sunglasses out of her purse. "I've been talking and standing all day at the conference."

"How did your presentation go?"

"Very well! I received very positive feedback. And I made some good contacts."

"I'm glad it was worth flying out here. All the hassle."

Grace settled back in her seat.

Unfortunately, there was already a lot of traffic. Esther chewed her lips. "I don't know which way will be worse, 101 or 280. I think I'll take 280. I'm sorry I lost track of time."

"It's okay," Grace said, her voice tired. "I don't mind. It's just good to see you again." She sounded as though she might drift off to sleep.

Esther waited for the light to change.

There had been another Chinese student who'd left the program after a semester when her husband was offered a job in Florida or Georgia, someplace in the South. Esther could picture her still. A very beautiful Northern Chinese woman, with long, crow-black hair and delicate features. She'd been incensed about the novel Brooks had assigned her to read for their comp lit class on historical novels. Half the novels were in Chinese, half in English. *Such a dirty book!* the woman had said. Esther and the woman were waiting in the hallway before class. It was winter. They were wearing heavy coats. What was her name? Esther tried to remember. *He is sexually harassing me!* she'd said.

Esther had dismissed her anger at the time. The novel was acclaimed, after all. It had won some major award. Brooks had known of the student's misgivings and joked about them in class. Then it came to her. What Brooks had said. "Hao Yu thinks this is a 'dirty book' and I'm a dirty old man for assigning it." He'd made a pun using the student's name. "Is it hao yu or huai yu?" Is it good or bad writing? "You tell me, class. What is literature to some is pornography to others." Brooks had shrugged dramatically. He turned her complaint into a discussion topic about aesthetics and free speech. "We don't want another Cultural Revolution, this time in the United States." Everyone had laughed. Of course the class sided with free speech, with Brooks.

The class was roughly half Chinese international students, half American. Esther had been the only Chinese American in the program. They were all insecure. They all wanted the professor to think of them as sophisticated.

Esther was in her first semester of graduate school. She'd skimmed the novel. It was graphically sexual. She'd hated it too. It was the kind of tedious book filled with the sexual fantasies of white men that was favored, unsurprisingly, by her white male professors. But was it sexual harassment to be assigned to give a report on a commercially published book that everyone else in the class had to read too?

Hao Yu was a very beautiful woman, and because of her beauty, Esther had meanly suspected at the time that she had a way of assuming all men were interested in her sexually.

Now she could see how Brooks had enjoyed embarrassing the woman. Esther remembered how she'd blushed through her presentation. How red her cheeks had grown as Brooks mocked her for being provincial and a prude. Esther had not defended her. Esther had not mentioned that she'd hated the novel too.

■ ■ ■

It was stop-and-go through Palo Alto, but then the traffic cleared once they were on 280.

"Oh, good! It's not bad," Esther said. "Maybe we're going to catch a break today."

Grace roused herself and looked out the window.

"Wow, this is very rural," she said. "It's not what I imagined."

She took off her sunglasses and peered at the green leafy trees on both sides of the interstate, the expanse of fields.

"I know, right? Look at all this open space!" Esther said, gesturing at the tree-lined fields on both sides of the highway. "Who owns this? This could be houses. This could be apartment buildings."

"Even if they build houses here, people like us could not afford them," Grace said. "They will still be very, very expensive."

"True," said Esther. "Still, I think they should try to build more affordable housing. People don't need any more mansions."

"It's not how the rich think," Grace said. "I teach their children. I know."

The sparse traffic continued for another twenty miles, and Esther even imagined there would be time to take Grace on a little driving tour of San Francisco before dinner. Then ten miles from the city, they rounded a bend and it was bumper-to-bumper. "Oh, shit," Esther said.

She craned her neck as though she'd magically be able to see through the wall of barely moving vehicles. "I'm sorry," Esther said, sighing. "I should have taken 101."

"I can't believe Brooks married that woman," Grace said, her voice a tight string, surprising Esther with its surge of anger. "Did you ever meet her before you left? *Eileen*," Grace practically snarled. "She was from Singapore."

"I heard about the wedding," Esther said cautiously. In fact Esther's father had sent her clippings. There had been a big write-up in *World Journal*, pictures of the famous Sinologist and his beautiful new wife. Esther's father had circled Brooks's head with a red marker and written in the margin: *This your professor?* The couple had had a wedding banquet with the bride's family in Singapore. From the pictures, it seemed Brooks was older even than the bride's father.

"After they were married, she moved into his house," Grace said. "I went to say goodbye to Brooks, and he told me, 'Go tell Professor Kwok goodbye.' He made me walk to the very back of the house. Eileen was sitting in his office, writing at his desk. He made me call her 'jiaoshou.' She didn't even contradict him." Grace shook her head in disgust. "Eileen was just a student, the same as the rest of us. She was never my professor!"

"You don't need him," Esther said, but as soon as the words left her mouth she was aware how inadequate they were. Of course Grace didn't need Brooks. But how much easier her life would have been. Being married to a famous professor, to an American, to security. His current wife had seen the advantages too. Why else marry a man a generation older than oneself?

"I'm sorry," Esther said.

"American women have all the power," said Grace bitterly, despite the fact that Eileen was Singaporean, not American.

Esther wondered if some of Grace's anger was directed at her too. Esther was American-born after all. She hadn't been pressured by Brooks for sex. Esther thought Grace's anger misplaced, directed at women instead of at Brooks, but Esther didn't see how she could point this out without upsetting Grace.

Grace crossed her arms over her chest and stared straight ahead at the grim line of red taillights before them. She sat like that, silently fuming, until they came upon the overturned truck that was causing all the traffic to back up. Acrid, black smoke billowed from the cab. There were police cars and flares on the road.

"I hope no one was injured," said Esther.

Then she saw the motorcycle that had been struck. It was partially flattened. Broken glass and bits of metal lay scattered across the highway.

"Look!" Grace said. She pointed to the side of the road, a metallic blanket stretched over a mound, over something. "That must be the body."

"I wonder if the motorcycle caused the accident," Esther said.

"Yes," said Grace, brightening. "Yes, it probably did."

The traffic thinned after that. Everyone had been slowing to gawk at the body.

They made it to Japantown before the Saturday night drinking crowds. Esther and Grace found a table at the new ramen place without any problems. Grace ordered sake for them both, and even though Esther didn't like to drink, and she was driving, she didn't feel she could refuse. Then after a couple drinks, Grace was laughing again, and Esther could relax.

Esther suggested they go to the karaoke place in the Kinokuniya Mall, but Grace said she was tired. She had to get up early for Super-Shuttle for her flight. So they went back to Esther's small apartment.

"I'm sorry. I don't have room for a couch. You'll have to sleep on the floor. But I've got a futon in the closet."

"It's okay," Grace laughed. "You should see me! I have to take students on camping trips. I've slept on the ground in a tent. I've slept in a cave."

"A cave! Oh my!" Esther exclaimed as she dragged the futon into the room.

"Oh, yes. A futon is luxurious for me!"

Grace lay back against the rolled-up futon, her legs stretched out before her. Her face was bright red from drinking. Esther imagined hers was the same. Instinctively she touched her own inflamed cheeks.

Grace yawned. "You know, I really like the cover of the Ha Jin book. I recognized this image immediately. The braid down the woman's back. I used to wear my hair like this. In two braids." Grace laughed, remembering.

"During the Cultural Revolution, my classmates and I were sent to a village in Sichuan," she continued. Her eyes were closed, her body limp, but her voice grew stronger. "I remember the monkeys were terrible. They were so naughty. They climbed down from the trees. They ran though the village. They stole whatever they could. One day a monkey ran up and grabbed a classmate's schoolbag. He bowed down before the monkey in an exaggerated manner, begging the monkey king to return his bag." Grace smiled at the memory of the girl she'd been. "This is how I chose my American name," she said.

"How so?" Esther asked, not following.

"My classmate, he kept saying, '*Your grace, your grace*,' in English to the monkey king. The boy had a contraband English book, and we'd all read it. This is how you talk to the king and queen of England, we thought. It made us feel very fancy. Like we were very knowledgeable about the world.

"So when I was choosing my English name, I thought of this memory." Grace's voice became unexpectedly soft.

"Did you keep in touch with him? Your classmate?"

"Oh no, we never saw each other again," Grace said. "After I returned to Beijing, I don't know what happened to this boy." Grace turned her head, looking at the wall. Esther could not see her face, but there was something about the angle, how she held herself, so vulnerable.

"Don't fall asleep like that!" Esther warned. "You'll get a kink in your neck."

"I won't," said Grace, sighing.

Esther helped Grace unroll the futon, then brought her some clean sheets and a blanket. She turned on the local news while waiting to use the bathroom as Grace showered. The accident that had held up traffic on 280 had made the news. There was a picture of the wreckage taken from SkyCopter7. The reporter, a young Asian woman, leaned into the camera, her face aglow with excitement. Esther turned off the news.

Esther sat on the edge of her bed. She knew that Grace would never report Brooks. He would continue to be a respected professor of Oriental Studies, the tallest tree in his field, a poet who collaborated with famous Chinese poets, all men. He translated their works into English, they published his works in Chinese. His taste assured what the world read of Chinese literature. Chinese women would continue to be his targets, and no one here or there or anywhere would do a thing about it. If anything, the women would be blamed for sleeping with a white American man.

When Grace emerged at last from the bathroom, her hair wrapped in a towel, her cheeks still flushed from the sake, Esther felt a rush of tenderness toward her friend. A lump formed in her throat.

"I'm sorry about Brooks," Esther said. "He's such an asshole."

"Yes," said Grace. She plopped down on the futon. Then she laughed. "I guess it's not a big surprise. I guess it's something I could have told you over the phone." She searched in her suitcase and pulled out a travel pack of tissues, dabbed at the tears forming in her eyes. She blew her nose. "I don't know why I felt so ashamed. So stupid."

"It's how you're supposed to feel," Esther said. "It's the patriarchy. It's how we're all supposed to feel."

"Yes, I know," said Grace. "Still."

They fell into silence, and Esther went to the bathroom to brush her teeth and change.

When she came out again, Grace was lying on her side on the futon, sound asleep, snoring lightly, the light still on.

Esther set the alarm on her dresser then turned off the light. She climbed into her bed. The world was spinning slightly. She opened her eyes and stared at the ceiling.

Suddenly she sensed that this was likely the last time she would see Grace. They lived so far apart. Their lives had taken them in different directions. Esther wrote grants for an arts organization. She edited their newsletter. It was okay as far as work went, but she wasn't in academia anymore. Their paths were unlikely to cross naturally.

Esther hadn't kept in touch with any of her old classmates apart from Grace. In fact, her memories of grad school were largely unhappy, memories of feeling inadequate, not smart enough, not driven enough. Brooks had mocked her accent, her vocabulary. "It's nice to have representation from the working class," he'd said once in class. She was intimidated by the credentials of her classmates who'd graduated from famous schools, whereas she'd merely grown up translating for her parents. They'd never gone to college, but they owned a restaurant in a small town. Who was she to imagine a life discussing literature? There had been a reading on campus, a famous novelist Brooks knew. Afterward, a party. The men had gotten drunk. Esther had been humiliated.

The unpleasantness had made her never want to return to these memories. It was how grad school was supposed to make you feel, Esther had assumed at the time, but she saw now that it was how men maintained their positions as the tallest trees in their fields, by chopping down any woman who might otherwise one day grow to be competition.

But who would believe any of this was harassment when it just seemed another part of the usual cruelty directed at women all the time?

Esther turned onto her stomach, then flipped onto her back. She couldn't fall asleep although her body felt tired. She listened to Grace's soft snores, the faint rumble of the Muni bus passing by on the street below, the sound of a man and a woman shouting somewhere in the distance as the moon traversed the sky. She watched its cold blue light sparking off her blinds.

Hong's Mother

. . . . .

Hong was nineteen and had been studying in France for three months when her mother called out of the blue.

"Guess what? I won the raffle at the St. Patrick's Day Gala!" Hong's mother's voice, triumphant, crackled over the phone line. "Tickets for two to Vegas."

"That's great," Hong said, wondering why her mother called just to tell her this. Long-distance calls were expensive, and Hong's mother hadn't called since she'd arrived in France in January. "That's kind of a weird thing for the church to be giving away."

"I asked Monsignor if I could convert the tickets," Hong's mother continued, ignoring her, "and he said I could. So I'm coming to visit you!"

"What? You're kidding!"

"No, I'm going to do it. I'm going to fly. You can pick me up in Paris. I'll come for your Easter break."

"Ah," Hong said. "Okay." So she had received Hong's letter. She'd told her mother that she was going to Paris for Easter with her classmates.

"And then you can take me to see Lourdes."

"Ah," Hong said.

"Everyone in the prayer group was so surprised. They can't believe I'm going to fly."

Hong's mother promised to send Hong the particulars of her flights. Then she hung up.

Hong knew how her mother hated to fly.

Hong had spent the first nineteen years of her life sitting in the back seats of cars as her parents drove back and forth across the country. It took three days just to drive to New York for a wedding. A trip for a job interview in California was a week-long ordeal. On the one long plane trip they'd taken when she was eight, Hong's mother was terrified that the plane was going to fall out of the sky. She'd fussed constantly. At one point Hong's mother insisted that she smelled smoke and made the stewardess inspect all the lights in the cabin, so sure was Hong's mother that one of them had a short that was on the verge of bursting into flame.

Hong as a child sometimes wondered if her mother's fears might be about more than flying. She even wondered if they might have been about the racism, but she couldn't quite loop that loop, see how the two unconnected things—racism and a fear of falling from the sky—were related, even in her mother's mysterious mind.

There were the times, too, when Hong's mother was certain she was going to fall ill—a sudden wind would arise and she'd catch a chill, and the next day, Hong's mother would take to bed and refuse to rise. It fell to Hong to get her brother up and ready for school, drag him to the bus stop, make sure he did his homework in the evening. As she grew older, sometimes Hong had to make dinner for the family. Her father complained about her bland cooking, her brother whined about leftovers. Once in ninth grade after her mother had taken ill for a week on end, her father had taken all their dinner plates and smashed them one by one against the floor. Hong had made the same dinner every night for seven days—tacos with ground beef and Ortega shells from the box because that was the one hot meal she'd learned to make in home ec. Within seconds the meat and shredded lettuce and cheddar were sprinkled with broken glass, inedible.

Later Hong's father had apologized to Hong's mother. She overheard them talking in their bedroom. She'd been working on her geometry homework and had gone to get a glass of water when she'd heard their voices murmuring. She'd knelt outside their door to listen.

"I don't know what got into me," she heard her father say.

Hong thought she heard her mother say then, "It's all right. I should have gotten up. But I didn't feel well. I don't know what came over me."

"No, no, no," her father said. "Protect your health."

Their conversation had infuriated Hong. Why was her father apologizing to her mother instead of to Hong? It had been Hong who had cooked and been insulted, all her hard work ruined, no dinner that night, and on top of it all, she'd had to clean up the mess. She'd cried sweeping up the glass and tacos. She'd been hungry, and she liked tacos. She'd added spice to the meat, not from the package the way her mother did it, but spices out of the jars from the spice rack, the way the home ec teacher had taught. Each night she'd tried a different combination, trying to come up with the perfect blend.

On these nights, Hong decided it wasn't the racism. It was her parents. And she vowed to leave when she could. She started planning, keeping her grades perfect, taking the classes her teachers advised. When the time came, she applied only to faraway, out-of-state colleges, private schools with money for scholarships. She decided to major in a language neither of her parents could comprehend.

Still, her mother had found a way to follow her.

. . .

Hong couldn't sleep the night before her mother's arrival. She pictured her mother on the transatlantic flight, clutching the hand of the nearest stranger, drinking the little bottles of Harveys Bristol Cream she favored.

Then she nearly missed her mother at the airport. After Hong took the Métro to Charles de Gaulle the next morning, Hong got off the airport bus at the wrong stop. She wasn't used to the French habit of announcing the next stop at the current one. So when the bus pulled up at departures but the woman's voice announced, "Arrivée," Hong jumped in alarm, her ears ringing, and ran off the bus. Only when she saw the large block letters DÉPART on the wall did Hong realize her mistake, but the bus was already moving on, and she knew from experience that French bus drivers once started wouldn't stop even if she ran along the bus shouting and pounding on the side.

Hong rushed into the departures door, figuring she'd find her way to her mother's gate somehow so long as she was inside the airport. There were armed guards with long, black rifles stationed at the entrance and before the escalators. There had been a number of terrorist attacks in France the previous fall, trash cans packed with nails that would blow up, bombs placed on buses, things that didn't seem to alarm the French people Hong knew but did cause armed guards to be positioned at major public places. The guards glanced at Hong then looked away as she rushed past them and up the escalators.

A female guard called up to her, but Hong couldn't understand. Hong said, "Je cherche ma mère," and kept moving. No one followed her.

At the top of the escalators, Hong could see that she was clearly in the wrong place. There were no passengers at all. She was faced with glaring white walls and closed doors and empty chairs, and Hong wanted to cry, but then she could hear the high-pitched voice of one of those female gendarmes and then very distinctly her mother's overly loud, ears-still-plugged voice floating through the plexiglass walls. Hong took off in the direction of her mother's voice, and sure enough, there she was in a long, chic green-and-tan coat smiling as the Frenchwoman in a uniform was trying to shepherd her through a door into the arrivals section of the airport.

"My daughter is coming to get me," Hong's mother was saying.

"No, no, your daughter is not here. Here is wrong for you," the Frenchwoman said in a tentative English.

"Ma! Ma!" Hong shouted, waving frantically.

Hong's mother looked up and smiled happily. "There! There is my daughter. I told you she was coming to get me."

The guard looked shocked as Hong ran up, grabbed her mother's arm, and pulled her mother after her. "Let's go to the baggage claim," Hong said, and off they went.

Hong's mother later said she had followed a Japanese tour group into this part of the airport. "They seemed to know where they were going."

And Hong explained that she had gotten off at the wrong stop or she would have never found her mother.

Hong's mother found their fortuitous mistakes to be a sign that Hong would be able to take care of her just fine while she was in France, and Hong felt all the more nervous, knowing how close she'd come to missing her completely.

Still, she'd called Hong her daughter, and the Frenchwoman hadn't questioned this. Hong took that as a good sign.

. . .

Sometimes, growing up, Hong had wondered if her mother was embarrassed by her presence. The way all the white women in their town asked aloud if Hong were adopted, told Hong their stories of their cousins who adopted Korean babies or distant relatives in other towns who'd sponsored Vietnamese refugees in their churches. "Such beautiful children," these women would say, their sharp white teeth flashing in their mouths.

It was as though the church ladies couldn't imagine that Hong's mother, a white woman like themselves, had chosen to marry a Chinese man and had sex with him and given birth to two mixed-race children, Hong and her brother. Instead it was Hong in their eyes who looked as though she didn't belong. Hong had the dark, straight hair, the dark black eyes. Hong's brother, Henry, had wavy brown hair with golden highlights, green eyes, height from some long-ago forgotten ancestor. It didn't mean that the church ladies liked him any better for his passing, just that his presence didn't prompt the adoption stories the way Hong's did.

Perhaps worst for Hong was her mother's silence in the face of these stories. The way she'd drift away from the conversation, turn and walk away, leaving Hong alone with the white women yapping about some beloved Oriental adoptee.

. . .

They'd been an ordinary family in all the places they'd lived before, first in California where Hong's parents had met and married and where Hong and her brother were born, then in New York where Hong's father had accepted his next academic position. Ordinary until they'd moved to this very small town in the Midwest. Hong's parents had gotten tired of the congestion, of Hong's father's hours-long commute to and from New York City. So when the job offer came, Hong's father took it.

They hadn't expected all the stares. When they walked down the main street of the small town, cars slowed, the drivers craning their necks to look. Then the obscene letters in the mail, addressed to "The Chinaman" or "The Floozy." The kids in school with their ching chong jokes, with their fingers to their eyes pulling them slanted. The church ladies with their adoption stories. Henry's fights in school. It didn't matter that it was the other boys, the white boys, who started it. He was the one who was blamed.

Hong's mother began to take to her bed, suffering from mysterious headaches and chills.

Hong's father threw himself into his work. He attended conferences everywhere—always on the go. Sometimes he'd fly to three different cities in one week. At home he was angry. He locked himself into his office with his books.

Hong's mother joined a prayer group. When she wasn't at work at the little dress shop she opened downtown, she was with her prayer group. She began to refer to Hong as her assistant instead of her daughter. She began to speak in a high-pitched breathy voice. She laughed along when her friends made racist jokes after church, in the bingo hall over donuts and black coffee.

"Ma, you shouldn't," Hong would scold at home, but her mother didn't seem to be able to hear her voice. Her mother drifted away, into housework, or important phone calls, or she'd go for a walk. Returning, refreshed, her cheeks flushed, Hong's mother declared, "I needed that!" when she came in the front door and brushed quickly past Hong, who'd been waiting. In the kitchen, Hong's mother clanged pots noisily, or else she headed straight to her car, remembering a prayer group meeting, something urgent.

Hong knew deep down it had to be the racism, not her parents, but it felt like it was her parents, and especially her mother. Henry didn't want to talk to Hong about it either. Hong was whiny and weepy. She was a girl. She was a smart Asian-passing girl like all the ugly stereotypes, glasses and big teeth and no friends and all that, nobody Henry in his precariousness wanted to be talking to.

By the time she was eighteen, Hong had had enough of this small town. She applied for college far from home; she got a scholarship; she did not return for breaks; then she applied for the study-abroad program in France without telling her parents first. Her financial aid covered it.

■ ■ ■

A few days before Hong's mother arrived, Hong received an envelope from her father. Inside he'd sent six hundred dollars in cash and a note: *Be sure to take care of mom.*

It infuriated Hong that he'd risked sending cash in the mail. That, and the fact that he was still enlisting Hong in his Mom-is-a-fragile-girl enterprise in which he and Hong were to act as guardians for Hong's mother. It had been this way since high school when Hong's mother had started to detach, drift, praying for the disabled children she knew to walk instead of praying, for example, for the racists in their town to stop being assholes.

But Hong knew the money would come in handy. True to form, her mother had not brought any of her own, expecting Hong to take care of her.

To stretch the money as far as she could, Hong arranged their itinerary to Lourdes in the cheapest way possible, which turned out to involve changing a grueling number of trains.

"Can't we rest?" Hong's mother said on the platform in Bordeaux as Hong urged her to hurry to make the next train. "Can't we enjoy the view?"

"You wanted to go to Lourdes," Hong said. "This is how to get there."

Hong wouldn't let them stop until they'd reached Bayonne. The buses that ran to Lourdes wouldn't leave until the next morning, so she found a small hotel and checked in.

There was a café attached. By the time they were seated, the sun was setting and the burly men on the street were making nasty-sounding remarks to each other in a patois Hong didn't recognize.

Hong's mother opened the menu and pointed to a dish. "What's this? I want to try this."

Hong had no idea what it was. Her French, she'd discovered sadly, was only good for reading novels in class; she had difficulty speaking to people on the street, reading menus, anything practical. "Some kind of sheep meat," Hong said, consulting the small dictionary she carried in her backpack. "I think we should stick to the chicken. Oh, they also have ham sandwiches," Hong noted, relieved at the familiar jambon on the menu.

"No, I'd like the mutton. I *love* mutton!" Hong's mother declared.

Hong was surprised. When had they ever eaten mutton in their family? Never. But now Hong's mother insisted, and so Hong ordered the strange menu item for her. Hours later, her guts roiling, her forehead feverish and sweaty, Hong's mother lay on the bed in their tiny room, overcome with food poisoning.

Hong ran to the bar on the street level to use the phone, and the tough Basque men mocked her on the sidewalk. "Oh, ouais, 'Ma maman est malade.'" They imitated her voice in a high-pitched sickly way that sounded nothing like Hong's actual voice. Plus, Hong knew she'd said "ma mère," not "maman."

Hong raised her voice. "Ma mère a besoin d'un médecin!" She repeated this until the barmaid picked up the heavy black telephone on the wall and called a doctor.

Hong's mother recovered. Perhaps a doctor made a house call and supplied her with enough antibiotics to reassure. Perhaps she simply threw up enough to expel the poison from her system. Years later, the details lost, all Hong could remember was that she'd purchased a large two-liter bottle of Sprite to keep her mother hydrated.

· · ·

The next morning Hong's mother was weakened from the food poisoning, shadows under her eyes, but she still managed to dress up smartly in a matching navy knit skirt and sailor's top with a white bow.

"You look good, Ma," Hong said, watching her mother tease her hair in their hotel's small, darkish mirror.

"I bought it just for this trip," she said. "I mean, I'm coming all this way, to France. I thought I should look appropriate."

Sometimes Hong's mother broke Hong's heart. The way she could sound like a little girl. Not for the first time in her life, Hong felt she was failing her mother. She'd booked the trains wrong, she'd made her tired, she'd let her mother get sick. She wouldn't love Hong now, she thought. Her mother wouldn't ever love her.

The bus to Lourdes from Bayonne took a couple hours, and then Hong and her mother were walking slowly up the surprisingly steep hills (*It must be so hard on all the disabled pilgrims,* Hong thought), when Hong's mother looked around at all the tacky shops selling tchotchkes of the Virgin Mary, overpriced postcards, racks of rosaries made from shiny plastic beads.

"It's nothing like *The Song of Bernadette*," Hong's mother said, startled.

They followed the signs to the grotto at Massabielle, and then Hong glimpsed the line of pilgrims already snaking around the mountain. She thought incongruously of the trip they'd made as a family to Disneyland when she was five; this had all the lines except no rides.

Hong's heart sank, but something about all the other people waiting reassured Hong's mother. "I read in my guidebook that you can take a bath in the water for free," she said.

"I don't think that would be sanitary."

"Some people drink the water," Hong's mother added.

"Don't."

"I don't think I could do that. I think your father would say it was full of germs. You know how he is about germs."

"No, don't drink it. You've already had food poisoning once." Hong was genuinely alarmed.

"All I really want is some of the holy water to take home," Hong's mother said, and Hong could breathe again.

The line inched forward. The mountainside was covered with crutches and canes strung about on thick ropes. There was a placard claiming formerly disabled people who'd been cured had sent their crutches back to Lourdes in thanks. It felt to Hong as though they'd stumbled upon some ancient battleground or one of the lesser Grimm's fairy tales that never made it into the canon. Closer to the actual grotto, there were even a few antiquated wheelchairs parked and rusting by the newly paved sidewalks.

They'd been standing for hours, Hong's mind mostly blank, thinking only about the possibilities for lunch, when suddenly Hong noticed everyone around them was carrying their own empty jugs and bottles. *You have to bring your own bottles,* she realized. She looked at the line behind her and just knew they couldn't start over again.

"Wait here, Ma. I'll go buy some bottles." Hong took off running.

"Get enough for everybody!"

Behind her, Hong's mother was rattling off the names of her prayer group, but Hong refused to turn around, pretended not to hear that her mother thought of them even here when she was with Hong.

Hong ran back to the winding main street lined with tchotchke shops. The merchants could smell her desperation. A large Frenchwoman smiled, revealing crooked nicotine-stained teeth, and held up a plastic bottle emblazoned with a likeness of the Virgin Mary outlined in gold.

"Combien?" Hong asked

"Cent cinquante," she replied.

"Merde!" Hong exclaimed like an idiot. She couldn't pay a hundred fifty francs for one bottle. That was almost thirty bucks. She tried to calculate how much money she needed to save just for their meals before her mother flew home.

"Vous n'avez pas des bouteilles moins chers?" Hong asked.

The Frenchwoman sneered in disgust, shook her head, and turned her back to Hong. There were apparently few things more repugnant than a cheap American religious pilgrim.

Hong darted back and forth across the street, but all the shops had fixed their prices accordingly. So she jogged down an alleyway, figuring the farther from the grotto, the cheaper the prices. Finally, she found a tiny shop run by an African woman. The woman appeared to be bored of her job and sat glued to a small black-and-white television in the corner. She allowed Hong to bargain, and Hong managed to buy one Barbie-sized plastic water bottle shaped like the Virgin Mary and a large jug with a gold stamp saying Lourdes, France on the side.

Hong ran back. Her mother was at the front of the line, waiting while a group of five pilgrims knelt and prayed before the gaily painted statue of the Madonna set inside the grotto.

"Oh, you should have bought more like this." Hong's mother held the Virgin Mary bottle up to the light.

"They're horrible, Ma. And everything's too expensive."

Hong's mother was disappointed, but there was no time to go back. They had arrived at the miraculous grotto. They followed the tourists in front of them and knelt before the Mary statue, and Hong's mother prayed silently, moving her lips, while Hong tried to figure out how to fill up the bottles with the holy water.

She'd been expecting an actual pool of water that she could dip the bottles into, something mystical, like a secret pond in a shaded alcove. But instead there were rows of rather ordinary faucets, like something anyone could screw a hose onto to water a lawn. Hong tried turning one and it released quickly, as though regularly oiled.

Some of the holy water splashed and dripped onto the pavement. Hong looked up, anxiously expecting to see an angry flock of nuns descending upon her, ready to make her lap up the holy water so that not a drop was wasted, but no one was watching. Other pilgrims were filling up their bottles. No one else got suckered into buying the overpriced touristy crap except Hong. Worse yet, the Virgin's head was too narrow, so it took forever to fill the bottle. Then when Hong tried screwing the gilt plastic crown back on, she noticed the gold paint was flaking off already, exposing the dull white plastic beneath.

There was a line to go into the baths—which were indeed free— but Hong's mother decided she'd rather not. (*Thank god*, thought Hong.) And then it was over. There was nothing more to see.

Hong's mother was tired, the food poisoning taking its toll, so they returned to the bed-and-breakfast in Bayonne. Hong's mother was lying on the bed, resting with a hand over her eyes, while Hong tried to fit her water bottles in her carry-on only to discover that the Virgin Mary–shaped bottle leaked. The crown wasn't secure, and the bottle was dripping holy water onto Hong's mother's clothes.

Hong couldn't believe it. She'd managed to fuck up the whole point of the trip. Her stomach plummeted. She was a child again. They were in a restaurant trying to eat, and the white people at the table next to them were staring, full out just staring, and Hong and her brother felt like giggling, when Hong's mother said it was time to go, just go. They didn't even get to-go boxes, and on the drive back home, on the highway past the empty fields of long-harvested corn, the sky wide and empty and touching down on all sides like a giant inverted bowl, Hong's mother had another attack, the kind where she couldn't breathe. *"Slow down, slow down, you're driving too fast!"* she cried.

"I'm not driving too fast!" Hong's father shouted and sped up.

"Slow down, oh, slow down!" Hong's mother started crying, and she covered her face with one hand and braced the other against the dashboard, as though steeling herself against the inevitable crash to come. *"The children, the children!"* Hong's mother cried. *"You're scaring the children! Slow down!"* Hong's mother began to pray loudly, a rosary, starting in the middle: *"Hail Mary, full of grace, blessed art thou . . ."*

Hong's father shouted, *"Stop crying! How did I raise such timid children! Stop crying! You're too timid! You're no children of mine!"* Even though Hong and her brother were not crying. They were staring out their respective windows, not speaking. Hong wished the moment would end, had never occurred, even as time collapsed and it felt like the last time Hong's mother had gotten nervous, had gotten sick, and she hated that she was being blamed, that she was called the timid one. But deep down she thought it was true too. Because wasn't she timid? She should have yelled at those racists in the restaurant, *What are you looking at?* She should have mocked them, but she'd let them drive her family away, and now as her father shouted and her mother cried, she couldn't find her voice to yell as she wanted, to yell at her parents, and tell them, *Cut it out! What's wrong with you?*

Hong sat on the floor of the tiny hotel room, kneeling before her mother's carry-on, trying to wring out the clothes that had gotten soaked, laying the blouse and the pajamas on the back of the sole chair in the room, trying to shake off this familiar feeling of having failed to anticipate disaster that was making her think of her childhood all over again.

Then Hong remembered the two-liter Sprite bottle. It was still sitting where she'd left it on the flat wooden writing desk listing against the wall. She poured the rest of the Sprite out into the bathroom sink, congratulating herself on having reserved a room with its own bath, then washed the bottle out thoroughly, over and over again. "The Virgin Mary bottle leaks," Hong said. "I'm going to transfer the water." There was no way to dry it really, so some regular tap water was going to mix with the holy water. She wasn't sure if that jinxed things, mixing the profane and the magical.

"It's okay," Hong's mother said from the bed without opening her eyes.

Hong filled the Sprite bottle with the holy water and secured it tightly. Thank goodness its white plastic cap was leakproof. Hong shook it, turned it upside down over the stained porcelain sink to test, and nothing spilled out, not a drop.

"Remember, don't drink this," Hong said, emerging from the bathroom to pack the Sprite into the carry-on.

Hong felt the knot in her stomach unclench just a bit. She was not so useless; she may have just saved the day.

"It's too bad you didn't get more of those Mary bottles," Hong's mother sighed, her eyes closed. "Everyone will want those."

"It leaks! And they were too expensive, Ma," Hong said. "You have no idea. I had to bargain like hell just to get this one."

"That's my daughter. Never pay full price," Hong's mother said.

Then she laughed. "Do you remember when Mrs. O'Connell asked for a discount on the dresses for their daughter's wedding? And you told her—"

"I said we weren't getting a discount on our rent, so no."

"She still remembers that. She came up to me the other day after Mass, wanted me to special order her size in a skirt. I told her if she ordered the matching jacket, I'd throw in a scarf. And she said, 'Well, you wouldn't dare if that Hong were still here.'"

"She called me 'that Hong'?"

"Well, maybe she said Hung. She's always had trouble pronouncing your name. Your father and I never imagined people would have such difficulty when we chose it. I thought it was a pretty name—"

"No, I mean, she called me *that* Hong?" Hong said.

"Anyway, I told her you left and you don't have time to think about the dress shop anymore, so she needn't worry," Hong's mother said.

"What does that mean? I didn't just leave. I left to go to college. That's normal."

"Well, it's normal for some people."

"Ma, did you expect me to stay in that shithole town?"

"That 'shithole town' is my home too, you know." Hong's mother sniffed. She turned her chin and held her nose at an angle. "But I don't expect you to come back and visit me." Sniff, sniff. "You have your own life to lead. Your father is the one who's hurt since you abandoned the family."

"I didn't *abandon the family*. I'm in college. It's normal to go away to college! It didn't even cost you anything!"

"You're shouting. You and your father are always shouting. I have a headache."

Hong's mother shut her eyes and rubbed her temples.

Hong's heart was racing, and it was just like she'd never left home. It felt as though her heart were going to explode in her chest. Explode and explode and explode.

• • •

The next day Hong and her mother took the bus to the train station in Biarritz, but the train that Hong had bought tickets for didn't leave until late afternoon. Hong couldn't remember what she'd been thinking. That they might want to spend more time in Lourdes? That there might be something else to see in the surrounding towns? Hong wondered aloud if she should try to exchange them for an earlier train back to Paris.

Hong's mother was not particularly pleased with this idea. "Oh, more trains," she said. "Can't we at least go to the beach before we start all those trains again?"

"Sure," Hong said, feeling guilty, like a bad daughter, again. Always.

Hong remembered the walk from the train station toward the shore, the ocean hovering quiet and blue in the middle distance. Later, she wouldn't recall what she'd done with their luggage. Maybe left it at a hotel near the station? Was that even possible? Were there lockers at the station? The bags were not in her memory anymore, but she could see her mother clearly still. Hong's mother was once again wearing her navy-and-white knit sailor dress, the one she bought for the trip, her winter coat draped over her arm. Hong was wearing her long, magenta down coat. Hong's mother's blond hair was glowing in the sunlight, while Hong's own dark hair was pulled back with a scrunchie. At least no one was staring at them, whereas back in the U.S. in their small town, even after all the years that they'd lived there, people had still stared at Hong and her mother and father and brother when they walked together down the sidewalk. Hong had learned to stand apart from her family, trail behind, or else to walk as quickly as possible, as though she weren't part of them at all.

Hong began to think maybe it wasn't her mother who had first drifted away. Maybe it was Hong who had chosen to leave her mother behind.

But in Biarritz, the chic French people walking on the boardwalk did not so much as glance their way as Hong and her mother walked toward the ocean.

It felt quite chilly, but Hong's mother declared that the breezes there felt like spring indeed.

"Let's sit on the sand," Hong's mother said. "Feel this sunshine! Doesn't it feel good? Oh, it's been so long since I've seen the ocean!"

They didn't have a blanket, but Hong's mother spread her green-and-tan overcoat onto the sand, and Hong plopped down next to her. Hong hugged her corduroy-clad knees to her chest and buried her chin into her collar because in reality it was still quite cold in early April. Hong's mother tilted her head back and let the sunlight brush against her cheekbones and her long, straight nose.

Apart from the two of them, it was mostly locals on the beach, it being too early in the season for tourists. Some young people set up a net for a game of some sort, an older couple strolled by hand in hand, children chased a luxuriously coiffed spaniel.

Their beautiful, soft, southern-inflected voices bobbed on the air, blending with the cries of the gulls, so that it seemed to Hong as though the birds were calling to each other in French. Then a family strolled onto the sand and set out their towels. The mother and daughter sat a few yards from Hong and her mother; both were fair-skinned with reddish-gold hair that glowed coppery in the sunlight. Hong watched as first the mother, then the daughter—who seemed about thirteen, fourteen—shed their jackets, then their tops, and finally they unhooked their brassieres and sat topless facing the ocean.

In the picture in Hong's mind, Hong and her mother sat perfectly parallel to the French mother and daughter like reflections in a long, angled mirror.

Hong's mother smiled, turned toward Hong, laughing, embarrassed. "Oh, can you imagine?"

"I would die," Hong said, huddling over her knees. It was mortifying to imagine herself or her mother naked and observed on a beach, and especially together.

Hong's mother put a hand over her eyes, shielding them from the sun. "Should we try?"

"What?"

"You know." She giggled. "When in France . . ."

"Mama," Hong said.

Hong's mother began to strip off her clothes, first her heels, then her hose, then her skirt and sailor top. Hong thought she'd stop, but she unhooked her bra and placed it neatly under the pile of her things.

"Come on," Hong's mother said. "Spoil sport."

Without waiting, she walked off toward the sea in her half-slip.

"Don't leave your purse!" Hong called.

Hong didn't know what to do.

She jumped up and tore off her sneakers, her socks, then her coat, her cords, her sweater, her button-up blouse, the T-shirt she wore under the blouse for extra warmth, and then, goddammit, she took off her glasses and tucked them into her mother's purse, and stuffed all her clothes in a pile under her coat on top of her mother's coat.

Blind, Hong squinted at her mother's blurry form retreating into the ocean. She ran across the sand in her saggy underwear, her mother's heavy leather purse hooked over her shoulder. "Don't forget your purse!" Hong shouted.

Hong's mother was already at the edge of the surf when Hong caught up to her.

The wet sand was freezing under Hong's toes and made her nerves jump as though she'd tripped a live electric wire.

A stream of clear water came rippling up the beach and splashed across her feet, her calves.

"Oooh! Oooh!" Hong's mother squealed.

Hong shouted as the icy water hit. The water was cold enough to feel metallic, like a knife stabbing her flesh.

Hong's mother laughed and grabbed Hong's arm. She nearly knocked Hong off balance and into the sea.

"Let's go," Hong said. "It's cold."

But Hong's mother pulled her toward the ocean. Hong's mother stood with her arms outstretched, her face tilted to the sun, as though she could embrace the sky.

Hong squinted at the shining ocean. A larger wave was coming their way.

"No, no, no!" Hong shouted as the icy wave hit.

"Oooh! That's cold!" Hong's mother clung to Hong's arm, as the water surged and foamed around their knees. And then another wave hit, higher.

"FUCK!" Hong gritted her teeth. Her vagina clenched. Every goose pimple on her body stood erect.

Hong could feel the water pulling back, retreating into the ocean.

"Let's go, let's go, let's go!" Hong pulled her mother with her; Hong's mother was laughing and shivering and nearly made Hong trip, but Hong managed to half drag her across the sand back to higher ground. The world was a blur, the sand a golden mass, the French people columns of light, the distant buildings smudges on the horizon. Hong found their pile of clothes on the sand when she stumbled across them and fell.

Hong's mother was still laughing. "Oh, that was fun! I've missed the ocean!"

Hong grabbed her mother's clothes with one hand. "Here," Hong said. "You're going to get sick."

Hong threw on her down coat without drying herself, then turned to help her mother.

She found her glasses in her mother's purse and then her T-shirt on the sand, and used it to wipe her mother's body dry. Hong's mother was shaking from the cold.

"Don't blame me if you get pneumonia," Hong said. "Don't blame me for this!"

Hong's mother's teeth were chattering as she put her bra back on and then her sailor top.

Hong held her mother's coat open as a kind of shield, in case anyone was watching. Hong refused to look at any of the French people on the beach, as though not seeing them would mean that they could also not see her as she helped her mother dress.

She held her mother's arm as her mother pulled off her wet slip then pulled on her knit skirt over her bare legs.

After Hong's mother had finished dressing, Hong threw on the rest of her clothes, stuffing the now-wet T-shirt and her mother's sopping slip into her mother's purse.

Hong's mother was still shivering as she clung to Hong's arm as they walked up the beach together.

"Your purse is so heavy," Hong said, shouldering it on her right arm, as she held her mother up with her left. "What do you have in it?" It felt as though she were carrying a cannonball.

"It's always this way," Hong's mother said.

Later Hong would think of all the times she'd seen her mother carrying her purse, basically her entire life, and never thinking to ask what was inside, never imagining the weight of it, just seeing it there, hanging off the crook of her arm like an extra limb.

They made it to the boardwalk, and it was a little warmer farther from the ocean and the sea breezes. There was a café across the street, and Hong suggested they get some hot coffee.

"Oh, no," Hong's mother said. "I need a drink. You'd better order me some red wine."

Hong was surprised. "I thought you didn't drink."

"Hurry up," said Hong's mother. "I could catch pneumonia."

Then the old white-haired French man at the door smiled at them both. *"Bonjour, mesdesmoiselles.* Such beautiful mother and daughter," he said in English.

"What makes you think we're related?" Hong said, out of spite.

"Oh, I can tell immediately. You both have this—" and he made a gesture with his right hand, circling his face, round and round. "Such beautiful round moon faces," he said.

And Hong's mother giggled like a schoolgirl—no, Hong realized, like a grown woman used to flattery, who knew how to respond to a man's charm—and Hong followed the maître d' and her mother to a small square table at the window, silenced. *Round moon faces!* she thought, and immediately she knew this was true. Her mother and she did share the same round face. It was the one thing about her mother that was not completely Caucasian looking, and it was the reason Hong secretly suspected that she had turned out so Asian looking, despite being half. She had her mother's moon face.

■ ■ ■

Over the years, Hong and her mother continued to have some problems, some smaller than others, some larger, but their relationship had taken a turn; there was no more running away for Hong. She returned to her family for major holidays. Wasn't this what normal families did? Besides, Hong had decided in college there was no such thing as normal anyway.

If Hong still felt not quite at peace with her mother, there was acceptance. Hong no longer pined for another, fictitious woman, the loving, rational, and self-reliant one Hong had dreamed her mother might become someday when Hong was younger, when fleeing seemed the only option for dealing with the pain that fluttered under her ribcage. Hong's mother, on the other hand, still complained at times about Hong, as though complaining might produce the compliant, pious, and simple daughter she had expected Hong to become, rather than the distant, rational, and self-reliant woman that Hong's mother found herself stuck with, but that was another story.

Hong's mother would sometimes allude to their trip to the beach, although to Hong's knowledge, she never let on to her father or brother what they'd done. She'd say things like, "When in France, do as the French," and Hong's mother would bring out a bottle of red wine that she'd purchased just for Christmas dinner. Or she'd serve éclairs after the Thanksgiving turkey instead of pumpkin pie, and say, "This is how the French celebrate." Then she'd look to Hong with a wink, and Hong would nod, "Yes, that's how the French do it."

"Well, you would know," Hong's father would say. "Hong studied in France and Eileen visited her there. They went to Lourdes!" And there'd be no more debate, no complaints from Henry about missing pie, because you couldn't argue with such expertise.

White Rabbits

. . . . .

Y e-ye always had a pocketful of White Rabbit candies for me when I was a child.

The first time, I was three, maybe four. Ye-ye put a White Rabbit in the palm of his hand, then quickly closed both fists, shook both hands, and opened them. The candy was gone. Then he closed his fists and had me pick one.

I tapped a knuckle, and he smiled. He opened his hand, and there lay the White Rabbit.

Who could resist? The white wrappers with the red and blue bands, the outline of the rabbit on the side. I untwisted the wrapper and found another piece of clear plastic around the white taffy, which I tried to peel off, but Ye-ye shook his head and showed me how to put the candy on my tongue. Miracle of miracles, the "plastic" wrap began to melt. It was paper made from rice paste, and it dissolved like a communion wafer on my tongue, revealing the sweet taffy beneath. This was what love tasted like when I was three: like magic and sugar and pounded rice paste.

My mother and father didn't want me to eat candy. They said candy would rot my teeth out. But eating White Rabbits was a religious experience for me now. There was no turning back.

Ye-ye didn't have any teeth. He wore dentures, which he put in a glass beside his bed at night to soak. I saw them floating in the glass free of his mouth when he spent the summers with us in our house in Southern California after my brother, Nathan, was born. Nai-nai had died that spring, and my parents thought Ye-ye would be lonely. I also think they knew he would be willing to look after me for free. My mother was tense and tired, and everything I did made her upset. I thought that would eventually change after the baby grew up a little bit, after the crying stopped or grew less frequent.

The moment I woke up, I would sit up in my bed and wait for Ye-ye to come, the second earliest riser. He'd peek into my room, and I'd hold up my arms, and he'd come and pull me out of bed.

Ye-ye took me for walks in the ancient stroller. The dew still glistened on the lawns, the air had a faint chill. He'd walk me to the corner and back, all by ourselves. We felt daring in the world.

This arrangement continued for years. Ye-ye coming for the summer, my brother taking all my mother's energy.

Ye-ye and I only got lost once.

By then I was six, and Nathan had an earache. It seemed to last the entire summer. He cried all the time. Mama was irritable. Everything I did made her tense. Same old.

We began as we always had. Ye-ye and I walked hand in hand up the shaded sidewalks before the sun had risen high enough to burn the dew off and scorch the air. Then we went a little farther than usual, all the way to the corner, and then across that street, and up the block to the big house with gray turrets and large dense fruit trees. The owners were an elderly white couple, and they had pomegranates. I'd gone on a field trip for kindergarten, and I remembered the way.

The nice couple had picked pomegranates from their trees and sliced them open and placed them on picnic tables covered with plastic red-and-white tablecloths. We'd all been given a quarter pomegranate to suck the seeds out of.

It was morning and I was hungry, and who knew when my mother would get up and make breakfast anymore.

"I know a good place to go," I told Ye-ye, and we set off.

But when we got to the corner, I could see the house but it was nothing like the friendly welcoming home of my memory. The tall wrought-iron gates were not tied open with streamers; there were not lines of elementary schoolchildren on the lawn with paper plates in their hands. The house was dark, shadowed, the pomegranate trees overgrown, the shade dripping from the eaves and the leaf-laden branches menacing. Even the spiky turrets of the house, which had made it seem castle-like on the field trip, now appeared threatening, as though a witch instead of a princess might live inside.

I froze in place, Ye-ye's warm hand in mine.

A bird cawed overhead. Some kind of jay. It flew into the tree, then seemed caught in the sticky darkness. Its cawing turned distressful, a shriek.

I squeezed Ye-ye's hand. He patted my head.

Ye-ye looked left and right. I knew he was wondering which way to go.

At first I couldn't move, then all at once, I knew we needed to run.

I pulled Ye-ye's hand, and we turned, crossed to the sunny side of the street. I knew there was another way home. A way only in the sunshine.

There was a little girl, Karen, whose house I'd gone to for a birthday party. I could picture the house, white with blue shutters and an orange tree and a Big Wheel on the lawn. I felt certain we could reach it. I had walked to the house with Mama pushing Nathan's stroller.

We walked another block. Ye-ye followed me, patiently, trusting me.

The sun was moving higher in the sky, the shadows retreating, but I didn't feel safe yet from the inky, shaded, witchy house. We walked and walked. And then I was lost.

I knew we should turn. We turned and turned, but what should have been our street, our house, our copse of avocado trees, was a different house, one with a chain-link fence and a large German shepherd with nicked ears staring through the wire. The dog barked, his harsh voice like electric volts to my heart.

Ye-ye felt it and gripped my hand too tightly; it hurt my fingers, and he pulled me along, but he couldn't walk very fast. Still he pulled me alongside him, and I didn't dare say *Ouch*, until we were out of range of the dog, a block and a turn away. We could hear the echo of his bark, but he was nowhere to be seen, and he surely couldn't see us either, I hoped.

We were truly lost then.

There was an old white man on a lawn chair in front of one of the houses. He wore shorts and an undershirt, and his belly poked out from his shorts. He held a limp hose in one hand. Water trickled from its mouth.

There were patches of dirt on his lawn, and dandelions, the kind my father would not tolerate on ours. The moment a single one appeared, Papa would march out with his garden spade and his thick gloves and a plastic trash bag, and he'd dig the dandelion up, all the way to the root, and bag it, tie the bag, and put it in the trash barrel before it could spread, he said. We were one of only a handful of Chinese families in our town in those days, and Papa felt it was important to show everyone that we understood the rules, that we knew how to keep our lawn nice, that we belonged.

The white man stared at us, and Ye-ye hesitated. I knew he was thinking we could ask the man for directions, but I didn't want to. I was afraid of the man. I prayed in my thoughts, *Ye-ye, no, we can't stop here*. Ever since I was very little, before I could talk, I knew if I thought hard enough, Ye-ye would hear me and understand.

No, Ye-ye, I prayed. *We can't stop.*

Ye-ye understood, and we kept walking.

The sun was very high overhead, and it was hot. Ye-ye was wearing his long-sleeved jacket, and he stopped and took it off, and folded it into half, and half again, and tucked it under his arm.

He took my right hand again in his left. My hand was hot and sticky and sweaty, but still he held me tightly.

We walked until Ye-ye suddenly had to stop on some stranger's lawn. He led me to a large shade tree, and he leaned his hand against the trunk. He took out his white handkerchief and wiped his face and neck and then the top of his head.

We were standing on the grass, which white people would not like. I knew from experience when my best friend, Gabby Ocampo, and I ran across the mean neighbor's lawn next to Gabby's house, and the old white woman had run out and shouted, "You brats get off my lawn!"

Ye-ye sat down on the lawn and patted the grass so that I would sit next to him. I was afraid we were going to get in trouble; there were white people in the house, looking at us through a crack in the curtains of their front window. I saw them flickering there, the curtains rippling back and forth. But I obeyed and sat on the grass.

Ye-ye reached into his jacket pocket and pulled out a handful of very melted White Rabbits.

Ye-ye's eyes twinkled as we both sucked on our candies, resisting the urge to chew, him because it was bad for his dentures, me out of solidarity. Except at the last minute when I absolutely couldn't stand it and I had to chomp on the candy until it was gone.

Then like magic, Papa and Mama drove by in our Buick. They were driving slowly, all the windows down, and I saw them and jumped up and ran toward them.

Mama shouted, "Ning-ning, don't run into the street!"

And I froze in place.

Papa parked the car right there in the middle of the street. He jumped out of the driver's side, and I thought, *We are saved!*

Then he ran over to me and swatted me on the ass, once, twice, three times. "Bad girl!" he said. And swatted me again.

I was too old for this. It wasn't the pain that made me grimace and fight back my tears as I stood there on the sidewalk in front of Ye-ye, in front of the white family who were watching from behind the curtains of their picture window. The indignity.

Papa dragged me by the arm to the car. He opened the back door and said, "Get in!" Then he pushed me inside and I sat down, even though the hot vinyl burned the back of my legs.

Then Papa went to get Ye-ye, and he helped him up slowly. He took his arm and walked him to the other side of the car.

Mama said, "Poor Ye-ye. Oh, poor Ye-ye. He could have had a stroke in this heat." Nathan was on her lap, and he started to whimper.

Ye-ye said something to Papa in Chinese that I couldn't understand, and Papa said something in Chinese back, only very loudly, and over and over.

Then Mama said, "Ning-ning, what were you thinking?"

That's how it was, ever since Nathan was born. I was blamed for everything that went wrong. His illness, his crying all the time, his having to go to the hospital, all the tests, all the doctors.

"Ning-ning, I'm ashamed of you. You know you're not supposed to leave the house alone. What has gotten into you?"

And I felt like saying, *But I wasn't alone. I was with Ye-ye.* But I didn't say it. Which turned out to be a good thing, because the next thing Mama said was, "You could have gotten Ye-ye killed. You're lucky we found you."

And that's when I cried for real, tears and snot and shame, in front of everyone.

■ ■ ■

After that, my parents became fearful. I wasn't allowed to go out by myself, and I wasn't allowed to go on walks with Ye-ye.

"He's forgetful. He's not himself. You're too much for him."

The next year, Ye-ye didn't come for the summer at all. He stayed in his apartment in New York City with my uncle. In fact, he wouldn't visit again in person ever. Traveling had become too hard for him.

However, he continued to send me White Rabbits in a box for my birthday and New Year's, along with a red envelope, every year until he died when I was eleven.

．．．

I didn't have White Rabbits again until I went to China on a study-abroad trip my junior year of college.

In advance of Spring Festival, the street stalls were suddenly full of bins and bins of White Rabbit candies. Walking the streets around the campus of Nanjing University, I was thrilled to see the candy of my youth. I immediately bought a bagful and brought them back to the dorm.

I passed them around to everyone I met. "I loved these when I was a child," I explained.

The old man who sat in the guardhouse at the gate politely took a handful, but the women who worked in the building merely shook their heads and laughed uncomfortably.

My Chinese roommate looked on in horror. "My grandmother liked those," she said.

I knew I was a disappointment to her. This whole mixed-nationality roommate situation was an experiment on campus, a sign of China's emergence from decades of seclusion, and was supposed to be an honor. My roommate had signed up and gone through some kind of rigorous screening process. She had been promised an American, and she'd expected some chic, blond white girl with exotic ways, and instead she got me, a Chinese American with cheap taste.

Back in our room she pulled out a Toblerone roll from the drawer of her desk and popped a piece in her mouth to make her point.

．．．

I'd come to Nanjing hoping to find some connection to my past, something that would perhaps console me, make up for the losses, for the sense of something missing in me, the hole that was always there in my life in America. But I was no fool. I knew that my grandfather was dead and the China of his memories was gone too, and the Chinese who lived now were rapidly throwing off the past and embracing a future of their own creation. Nothing in China was quite what I'd expected or hoped for.

After my roommate's scornful response, I kept my fetish to myself. But every morning when I woke, the loudspeaker outside our window blaring music for the morning exercises that my roommate and I refused to rise for, I reached from the cocoon of my comforter into the frosty air of our unheated dorm room and pulled a new White Rabbit from the bag I kept on my desk. I untwisted the familiar wrapper and popped the candy into my mouth. Pulling my comforter around me, I closed my eyes as the sensuous layer of sweetened rice paper melted into the milky taffy and braced myself for the new day.

Jia

· · · · ·

Mom grabbed her jewelry box, and her suitcase, and her purse, and then took Lu-lu by the wrist, announcing, "I've had it. We're leaving. We're going back to California. I want to see my family!" Mom ordered Lu-lu to get in the car and then backed down the driveway fastfastfast, their tires even squealed a bit, and then they were driving away.

"But I didn't pack any clothes."

"We'll buy you new things."

We don't have any money, Lu-lu thought, but she did not speak up for fear her mother might change her mind. It was exciting to be in the car, driving, the idea of leaving, leaving Dad and the house and the fighting, the shouting, Lu-lu's school with the girls who stared and wouldn't let her sit at their tables in the lunchroom.

Lu-lu didn't remember California. She'd been born there, and then her parents had moved to the East Coast when she was still a toddler, and then again to this small town in Indiana, but she was ready to go.

Mom never drank when she drove. When Mom drank, she just stayed in bed, complaining that her nerves were shooting sparks through her body.

Lu-lu pressed her feet against the floor mat as though she had secret pedals on the passenger side that could make the car move faster.

"I miss California," Mom said. "I never wanted to leave. Your father put up such a fuss. He said, 'You are holding me back! You are ruining my career!'" Mom cried, tears dripping off the tip of her nose. She wiped them on the back of her hand, pulled a crumpled tissue from the pocket of her coat. Dab dab dab. "But what about my life?" She said this louder than Lu-lu expected, a wail.

. . .

They used to travel every summer up and down the coast when Lu-lu was very small. They'd gone to Washington, D.C., to see the museums on the Mall and the Lincoln Memorial, all the way to Monticello in Virginia, another time to Fort Ticonderoga in upstate New York in time for the Bicentennial. Mom was afraid of flying, plus it was too expensive. They stayed in all the travel lodges, the HoJos and Super 8s and Motor Inns and motel chains so small no one else had ever heard of them.

Dad snored, and the noise amplified by the smallness of the motel rooms used to drive Lu-lu crazy. She couldn't sleep, listening to the deep inhale, the pause, and the teakettle whistles as he exhaled loudly through his nose, before the final gentle *poo* sound he spat from his mouth. "How can you stand it?" she asked her mother once.

"Oh, I got used to it." Mom had shrugged.

In those days, it was her parents' restlessness that drove the family. Lu-lu sat in the back seat of the car with her books and her dolls, ignoring their fights as they drove in circles, lost on the interstate, trying to find some new famous place they needed to see as a family.

Once when Lu-lu was seven, they drove all the way to Vermont with Ye-ye and Nai-nai in the car. Mom had wanted to see the autumn leaves. They normally didn't travel so late in the season, but Dad had agreed. He must have had some kind of break from school.

They picked fragrant apples in an orchard and ate them as Dad drove, Ye-ye removing the peel in a single long red thread with a knife. They all marveled at the whimsical signs shaped like black-and-white cows, the roadside stands selling fresh produce, buckets of yellow squash and orange pumpkins, the barns red as firecrackers against the green fields and the clear as water blue skies. Nai-nai had laughed with delight, exclaiming in Chinese and English that they'd somehow stumbled upon zhen shi de mei guo, "the real America," the America of old black-and-white movies and history books, home of the blond, blue-eyed Americans that they rarely encountered in the city or Jersey. It had been a magical trip, and it had given Dad ideas, a sense of the bigness of America. Why live so tight and small with this big, vast country out there?

The next year Nai-nai died, and then Ye-ye grew frail, then frailer. He couldn't sit in a car for their trips anymore, he couldn't live on his own, and then he went to live with Lu-lu's uncle back in Taiwan.

. . .

Every year after that, Dad applied for new jobs, for teaching positions with bigger salaries and administrative positions, until he got the offer at the college in Indiana. After they moved to their new small town with the big houses, Lu-lu wondered what Nai-nai would have thought. Their house was now big enough for her grandparents to live with them comfortably full-time, the way their house in New Jersey was not. But Nai-nai was dead, and Ye-ye was not coming back, even though her father still asked him every month when they talked on the phone.

"Is Ye-ye coming?" Lu-lu waited up, after midnight, just to ask.

"No, not yet," Dad said. But later she heard her father tell her mother, "He says he's too old. He doesn't want to move anymore."

But the next month Dad called his father again, describing the rooms in their new house, the space, the lawn, the big trees. "You would love it here, Ba." Then Dad said it: it was zhen shi de mei guo. Not the crowded city where they'd lived all those years after the war had ended and they'd first come to America, dependent on their sponsors, trying to rebuild their lives. "Hui jia," Dad implored. Come home. In Chinese the word for family and the word for home were the same: 家. Come home, come back to the family.

Dad kept asking, month after month, but Lu-lu knew Ye-ye would not love it here. It was Nai-nai who'd loved the green fields and the open skies on their trips, and Ye-ye had gone along with it because he'd loved her. She didn't know how to explain this feeling to Dad, however. Not in a way that wouldn't feel like she was blaming him.

. . .

Lu-lu knew it was her grandparents who'd chosen the characters for her name. For months, as her birth approached, Ye-ye and Nai-nai had written fervent letters to her parents in California, suggesting various characters, explaining the symbolism, the good fortune that each combination could bestow upon the newborn's life. Finally, they'd picked the characters, Lu, 鹿, meaning "deer," and ying, 英, "brave, heroic."

As a small child, Lu-lu had not understood when she'd been told what her name meant. *Brave deer?* It had made her giggle and prance around the living room, pretending to be an animal. Ye-ye and Nai-nai assured her it was a good name for a girl, but she wasn't really sure.

After her parents enrolled her in school, they discovered Lu-ying was hard for her teachers to pronounce, and soon they allowed them to call Lu-lu by her nickname—and it stuck.

After Nai-nai died and Ye-ye flew away, her true name was the only thing that kept her tethered to her grandfather.

When her father called Taiwan, he did not pass the phone to Lu-lu. Calls were expensive, and it was important to save money. Ye-ye was hard of hearing anyway. Her voice was too soft. Once, shortly after he'd first moved, when Lu-lu had picked up the phone, her grandfather had said, "Hello?" over and over and then hung up no matter that Lu-lu was shouting, "Ye-ye! Ye-ye!" He could no longer hear her voice, and he'd thought he'd lost the connection.

When Ye-ye wrote her twice a year, for her birthday and for the new year, he wrote her full name on the envelope in his beautiful handwriting, *Miss Lu-ying Chao.*

She put the letters in the envelopes in the bottom of her desk drawer for safekeeping, evidence of her true self tucked away for another day.

. . .

The road trips stopped after they moved to Indiana when Lu-lu was eight. At first they were too busy, or rather Dad was too busy, settling in to his new job at the college in their small, small town where people stared at them, specifically white people stared because they'd never seen a Chinese man married to a white woman before. In the other towns they'd lived in, closer to big cities in California and New Jersey, her parents' marriage had never been a thing that made people stop on the street, slow down their cars so they could turn their heads and stare at the three of them on the sidewalk or on the lawn of their new house—which Mom had been so happy about, because it was larger than any house that they'd ever been able to afford on either coast. "I feel like a celebrity," Mom had joked at first. But after the staring continued, she eventually stopped.

"It's nineteen-eighty-one, for pete's sake," Dad said.

They used to go to Indianapolis every weekend after they first arrived; it was only fifty miles north. Dad missed Chinese food so much, and their town didn't have a Chinese restaurant. They found a restaurant in Indy that Dad liked, not as good as the ones they'd found in Chicago, but Chicago was too far to go often. In winter, there were blizzards, the sky clouding over with the thick, fleecy clouds, and what started as flurries could turn to a blizzard with wind and snow that blew in all directions.

One Sunday in November, they'd driven home from Indy and been stranded overnight in a highway rest station two miles from the exit to their town. In the last twenty miles the storm had come up, defying all the meteorologists' predictions, and they'd crept along the interstate in a caravan of cars and trucks for hours, moving less than five miles an hour. After that, Mom didn't want to go anywhere. Everything made her nervous. The wind was too strong, the clouds were menacing, or the trucks were too fast, their drivers were reckless. "They're going to run us off the road," Mom wailed, covering her eyes with her hands, praying loudly. "Turn back, Walter!" she'd implored Dad. "Oh, let's go home!"

But if winter was bad, spring, summer, and fall were even worse. There were the thunderstorms that could flood the roads or turn to hail in a heartbeat or, worse, send tornadoes in funnels of death to wreak God's havoc on the wicked earth.

Lu-lu learned to read the sky; the greenish-yellow bruises appeared in the clouds, and she'd know a storm was coming and they could turn around in time, return to their home, safe.

When they were trapped in their town, her parents grew more tense, they argued, their voices circling the rooms of their house.

. . .

Someone in their new town dumped garbage on their lawn for three months until it started snowing. At first Lu-lu's parents thought it must have been the wind, knocking over their trash cans on the curb, spreading the trash from the torn bags for all to see. Funny that the rest of the neighbors' trash cans were in place. But the wind was unpredictable like that. And hadn't they all heard the wind after they'd gone to bed, rattling the glass in the windows, whooshing through the trees?

Then the next week it happened again.

Dad secured the trash cans in place with concrete bricks placed inside under the trash bags, with rocks on the lids, so there'd be noise enough to wake him, her mother, Lu-lu, if someone tried it again.

Then other people's trash started appearing on their lawn.

The first time, Lu-lu followed behind her father with an open Hefty bag as her father, armored up in gardening gloves and his Yankees cap, bent over and picked up the soggy empty packages of Jolly Green Giant frozen peas, cans that once held Campbell's cream of mushroom soup, the boxes of Kraft macaroni & cheese and no-brand corn dogs. Their neighbors ate crap, Lu-lu realized.

She glanced at the neighbors' houses, scanning for a crack in the tightly drawn drapes of the elderly couple who'd squinted at her without saying hello when they first moved in. Lu-lu remembered the green-and-yellow Mayflower truck parked in the street, the movers sweating in the August sun, piling the boxes onto dollies, and the elderly white couple across the street frowning from their living room. She surveyed the house with the wooden duck-on-a-stick in the lawn, with its wings that spun around in circles in the wind to drive away . . . what? Owls? Pigeons? Something that flew, Mom had said, but Lu-lu couldn't recall what now. The neighbors with the American flag decals all over their mailbox. Was she stereotyping them by judging their lawn decor? Did this mean she was a bad person? Lu-lu tried to remember what she'd been taught in CCD about judging people in her heart. Was there a special saint she was supposed to pray to for strength? But nothing came, her mind was empty as she watched her father fill the Hefty bag with other people's trash.

The next week when it happened again, Mom called the police. The police did not come to investigate. They did not rope off their lawn with yellow tape. They did not send an officer with a notebook to diligently take notes or a brush to dust the metal trash cans with powder that would reveal the culprits' fingerprints, with a blue light to catch hidden forensic evidence on the driveway. Lu-lu realized she'd watched too many cop shows on TV.

■ ■ ■

There was the staring. There were the catcalls shouted from the windows of cars, pickups. There were the racist jokes that white people would say in front of them. "I heard all the stray cats and dogs have gone missing in your neighborhood, Walt. Not cooking up anything special, I hope?" The transposed L's and R's. The jokes about height and shoe size, which even Lu-lu knew had something to do with sex. There were the jokes at faculty parties, after all the cocktails, that Lu-lu could hear from whatever side room she was relegated to with the other children. Often at these parties, she was put in charge of the children, which she thought was strange given her parents weren't the hosts. What new world had they stumbled into? Still, it was better to be in the side room with the little kids, sitting and watching movies on cable or directing them in games so they didn't fight. Mom was proud when Lu-lu was useful. Lu-lu could hear the jokes because the adults' voices were louder after they'd been drinking, loud enough to carry down the hall, over the clanking of dishes, under the closed door. Dad laughed the loudest, as though to say he wasn't bothered at all.

. . .

Once Lu-lu returned home early from a birthday party after she'd admitted during truth or dare, "Of course I'd kiss a girl—if I liked her," and then discovered there was no shaming bigots that their prejudices were unsophisticated and small when all it took was one stupid but popular girl to say, "Ew, gross! Homo!" for all the rest to join in laughing and snickering. She had wanted the consolation of home but instead found her parents shouting at each other in the kitchen. There were shards of glass on the linoleum mixing with meat and pasta and bits of iceberg lettuce. Mom cried, face in her hands, and Lu-lu grabbed the whisk broom under the sink, swept the mess into the small plastic dustpan and dumped everything into the trash. She moved so fast that her parents hardly noticed. Her parents stayed in the kitchen, arguing, while Lu-lu crept down the hall to her bedroom to finish her homework. They argued on and on, and she didn't emerge again, even though she was hungry, her stomach rumbling all night. It hurt her too much to see them attack each other.

There were more arguments in the months that followed. Vases were smashed. The jade tree that Ye-ye and Nai-nai had given her parents for their wedding was thrown against a wall, the plaster and wire trunk broken in half, the leaves chipped. Lu-lu remembered that her parents had promised the tree would be hers someday, when she was ready for college or an adult or something, some future date that now was never going to happen.

Lu-lu didn't confront her parents about their behavior and how it made her feel—small and ugly and worthless—because of the small, nagging and ugly feeling that perhaps her parents were in fact angry at *her*, were sorry she'd been born, were disappointed that she stood out racially from the other kids in this town, her features so obviously a blend of their own, which made them seem naive about their love, like suckers even. Lu-lu couldn't imagine how her parents had expected her to turn out, but their anger at each other made her feel responsible for not measuring up.

■ ■ ■

At thirteen, Lu-lu dreamed of nothing so much as leaving. When they'd first moved to Indiana, she had mostly hoped they'd go back to New Jersey someday, but after nearly three years away, she began to think of their old town in New Jersey less as their home and more as their former home, her old friends had new friends and wrote her less frequently, and she dreamed of a fresh start, a new place, a new home where no one knew them or who they had become—unhappy people shouting in their own home.

California sounded just fine, even if she didn't remember it at all, and Mom had wanted to leave her family behind because her father drank too much and her mother had been angry her whole childhood. Lu-lu knew her maternal grandparents through a single photograph taken with them when she was a baby and her mother's stories. But California, Lu-lu knew, was home too to the movie stars, to all the dark-haired women with smoky eyes that she was falling in love with: Sean Young with her *Blade Runner* shoulder pads; Maren Jensen who had battled the Cylons on *Battlestar Galactica*; Phoebe Cates who had a secret Chinese parent. Lu-lu clipped their pictures from magazines, pinning them to her walls so that she could gaze from their beautiful faces to her own plain one. She didn't have words yet for this feeling.

Maybe in California, Lu-lu thought, she would not feel so alone.

. . .

They made it to the edge of town, just before the exit to the interstate, when Mom pulled off. "We better get some gas," she said.

"We still have half a tank," Lu-lu said. *We can get gas at the next exit*, she thought, but she didn't dare say it out loud. Lu-lu never knew when her voice might set her mother on edge.

Lu-lu bit her lips and tried not to think, tried to turn herself completely blank so that she would do nothing that would irritate her mother. The sky was clear, free of clouds as far as Lu-lu could see, perfect traveling weather. Once she and Mom were gone, Dad would have to follow, and then they would all be safer. It seemed clear to Lu-lu.

"Well, I'm getting gas now! We don't want to be stranded on the highway. You wouldn't like that one bit, Missy," Mom said. Mom got out and slammed the door shut. She fumbled with the gas hose and nozzle. The wind tossed Mom's fine blond hair around her head. Mom turned her face directly into the wind, lifted her chin so that her hair was blown out of her eyes, the better to see.

It was cold out. All the trees along the side of the ditch had already turned from yellow to brown, or their leaves had already fallen, their branches bare, scratching at the sky. Snows would start soon. *Then how can we drive all the way to California?* Lu-lu thought. They should leave now. Now was still possible.

Mom threw open the door, and wind blew inside, chilling Lu-lu. Mom grabbed her purse, and then she stomped across the asphalt to the little convenience store to pay.

Lu-lu watched through the windshield as Mom talked to the clerk behind the counter.

The young man nodded his head, then he laughed. Mom was saying something funny or charming.

Mom kept talking. Lu-lu watched her mother's back, the way she moved her head, tossed it, patted her hair.

The sky darkened. A murder of crows swooped over the gas station and disappeared into the trees across the street. The car grew very cold, but Mom had taken the keys with her. Lu-lu's toes burned. She tapped her feet against the floor mat, faster and faster, trying to warm them.

There was a danger in joining Mom. Something might turn, might become Lu-lu's fault, but it was also possible that Mom had forgotten Lu-lu was there, waiting. Lu-lu got out quickly and ran into the convenience store. The door had a bell that rang when it opened, and both Mom and the clerk turned when she came in, her black-brown hair blown about her head, her cheeks flushed.

Mom turned at the sound of the bell, still smiling, but not at Lu-lu, happy, high from the conversation, the episode, mania, something.

The clerk stared at Lu-lu, narrowing his eyes.

"Mom?" Lu-lu said.

"Oh," said the clerk. He turned back to Mom. "One of my cousins adopted an Oriental baby. And they sure love her."

Mom laughed along, as though this was a special club they'd joined, she and the clerk's cousin.

"I'm not adopted," Lu-lu said. "I'm the product of my mother having sex with my father."

"Lu-lu," Mom said, "we're going to be late. We'd better go." She jangled the keys in her hand.

Lu-lu followed Mom outside again. She noticed Mom was carrying a brown paper bag, which she put quickly onto the floor of the back seat. Mom climbed behind the wheel of their Jeep and turned on the ignition. Lu-lu scrambled into her seat on the passenger side.

"Oh, that did me so good," Mom said, but not really to Lu-lu.

"Are we going to California?" Lu-lu said. Her voice came out as a croak, as though she hadn't spoken in years.

Mom was smiling at something Lu-lu couldn't see, something only Mom could remember.

Don't drink, Mom. Don't drink. Lu-lu thought about saying it out loud, but she didn't dare. If she said it, would Mom be angry? Would it ruin Mom's good mood and make her drink more? If she said it, and Mom drank, then it would be Lu-lu's fault. If Lu-lu didn't say it, then it might not happen.

Mom drove past the taxidermist shop, the used car lot and U-Haul rental lot, the Hoosiers Bar & Grill, and the Dairy Queen, which was dark, closed for the season. Mom drove past the high school track, the Frontier Savings & Loan, past the Kroger, the post office, the First Baptist Church, the Methodist church, and then the dog park, or what Dad called "the dog shit park" because people let their dogs run free and were selfish and terrible and didn't clean up after their animals.

Mom turned down their street. Dad had put on the porch light and all the lights in front of the garage.

"Don't tell Dad where we went," Mom said. "He doesn't need to know. It's not bad to keep him guessing sometimes. Our little secret."

Lu-lu eased up on the floor mat, lifted her feet. They were home.

Slow Train to Beijing

. . . . .

Lu-lu promised she'd attend the party at the engineering college, but already she regretted it. She didn't like such parties—the music was too loud, you couldn't talk, the partygoers were mostly foreign students plus some Chinese students who were friends with the foreign students. There were a lot of drugs. There was a huge underground that certain students knew how to tap into, and the cloying scent of hashish drifting from the dance floor was thick enough to compete with the coal dust in the air. The mere act of breathing was actually unpleasant.

But she'd promised to attend as a favor to one of the other American women who lived in her dorm. The woman was teaching in the city, at a different high school. The American teacher was dating a man whom she suspected of cheating on her, so she wanted to go to this party and either catch him in the act or confront him. The American teacher was somewhat afraid of the man and wanted Lu-lu there "just in case."

"You should just break up with him," Lu-lu advised, alarmed by the prospect of violence. She wasn't afraid—who would be so stupid as to try something in public, at a party with so many witnesses? The Chinese guards on campus tended to look the other way when it came to student parties, especially where foreigners were involved, but would they allow a foreign woman to be beaten at a party? It was December, and martial law had been underway for six months already. No one wanted more trouble.

Lu-lu was alarmed that her friend, otherwise so intelligent and capable, hadn't already broken up with a man whom she suspected might become violent with her. Cheating or no, he was a dud. Lu-lu said as much, but the woman said she needed "closure."

"Leaving him will be closure," Lu-lu said. But the woman wanted to talk to him; she wanted to talk where it would be "safe." ("Write him a letter," Lu-lu said.) The woman said it was important that she not allow herself to be used. She had to have this talk.

So Lu-lu went along with the woman, although she wondered what she could really do if something, anything happened.

They rode their bicycles across the city, and by the time they arrived, Lu-lu felt nearly frozen. There was no heat in the city in winter because Nanjing was south of the Yangzi River, the government's cut-off line for determining which part of the country was allotted coal for heat and which was not. Nanjing was, however, right on the banks of the Yangzi, only technically "in the South" but still in a very northern climate zone; it snowed on occasion and was generally wintery in winter. The government cutoff was arbitrary and just made people's lives more difficult. This was the kind of thing Lu-lu's Chinese friends grumbled about when they were alone with her and free to talk.

They rode up to the large brick wall and showed their IDs to the Chinese door guard. The American teacher only had to flash her work ID, but Lu-lu had to bring out her American passport. She knew from experience that her Americanness would be questioned. Chinese women going to foreign-student parties were always given a hard time. There had been riots because of Chinese women dating African students in the years preceding the student demonstrations at Tiananmen. The guards weren't going to risk anything dicey under martial law, so that meant they harassed all the Chinese and Chinese-appearing women going to the parties.

. . .

Lu-lu had complained about the double standard when she first arrived, but the other Americans had not been particularly bothered by it, and she eventually gave up complaining to them, even if it was something that still galled her in her heart.

Once inside the campus wall, they rode their bikes to the squat building where the party was already rollicking along. Even if they hadn't been given directions, Lu-lu suspected they could have found it from the sound of the bass booming through the walls and the smell of pot in the otherwise crisp night air. People tended to smoke twice as much in the cold, as though inhaling smoke would bring the fire's warmth inside their chilled flesh.

There were dozens and dozens of bikes jammed together at the racks. Lu-lu parked hers where she could hope to find it again, away from the other bikes under a listing pine tree, a little distance from the entrance.

Riding on the freezing cold metal for a half hour was like straddling an ice cube. She could barely walk now, her flesh burned from the cold. Lu-lu staggered bowlegged after the American teacher as though she'd just hopped off a horse, a horse made of solid ice, and stomped up to the crowds gathering at the doors to smoke regular cigarettes.

"Oh, I see him! The bastard," the American teacher said brightly, peering through the door.

"Shall I wait here?" Lu-lu asked, but the American teacher ignored her and pushed her way through the dancing throngs. Abandoned, Lu-lu sighed and decided to wait at the entrance. In case her friend needed to leave early, they'd be able to run back and get their bikes more easily.

"Can I have a cigarette?" Lu-lu approached a group of Chinese men clustered outside the doors, speaking loudly in putonghua. She tapped the shoulder nearest her.

Lu-lu was startled when the person turned and Lu-lu saw that she was in fact a woman. The woman was wearing a long, green soldier's overcoat, the kind sold in ordinary department stores, and she had chopped her hair off close to her ears. She was tall, taller even than Lu-lu, and masculine presenting from behind, but she had long feminine eyes and full lips and a slender nose. She did not look like the women in Nanjing. The woman said, "Help yourself" in putonghua, and there was just a slight accent that caught Lu-lu's attention.

"Oh, you're American," said Lu-lu. "Me, too. I'm Zhao Luying, but everyone calls me Lu-lu." Lu-lu offered the woman her hand, then immediately felt stupid. Who shook hands? What was she thinking?

But the woman shook her hand. "Call me Alex," she said.

So Alex it was.

They got to talking. The woman was from Los Angeles. She was studying in Beijing but visiting a friend in Nanjing. Lu-lu wanted to know about her life in Los Angeles, what had made her leave it to come to China. They talked, then they danced.

The dance floor was crowded, but they found a corner. At first they danced in a group with the circle of Chinese friends the woman had brought with her, grad students from the art college. They were all cool looking, wearing interesting clothes unlike Lu-lu's or the other students', some splattered in paint or cut in unusual ways. Lu-lu was surprised that they all seemed to enjoy talking to her (such was her self-esteem), that they liked her opinions on life in Nanjing and listened intently when she spoke of her job teaching in a regular high school and her night school classes that she taught around the city for under-the-table pay.

Alex leaned in once while Lu-lu was dancing and they bumped hips, which was silly and funny, an old disco move that they'd both been too young to appreciate when it first appeared in the '70s. The bump started a trend that took off across the room, and then Lu-lu was doing her best John Travolta impression, complete with finger pointed at the disco ball, a move that the Chinese students had apparently never seen before. The woman leaned in again and squeezed Lu-lu's arm, and Lu-lu felt her spine shiver.

Then the music changed, and it was harder to dance in a circle, so they dispersed. It was getting late and Lu-lu needed to get home. She had to get up early in the morning for an assembly at school.

She tried to find the woman she'd come with, but the American teacher was deep in conversation, not with the man she'd broken up with, but one of his friends, and although Lu-lu waved at her to let her know she was leaving, the woman did not notice, or else did not want to break her concentration on whatever her ex's friend was saying.

Lu-lu and Alex walked into the cold air, which was even colder now but bracing, free of the cloying marijuana smell. It almost tasted fresh when Lu-lu inhaled deeply.

"I'll ride with you back to your dorm," Alex said. "I'm staying near Nanda anyway."

It was late and the bicycle lanes were mostly empty. They saw a few workers riding home after a late shift, a few men slowly peddling bikes pulling flat carts loaded with baskets left over from the free markets, and then even slower bicyclists pulling long flatbeds loaded with small mountains of bricks or concrete blocks and one extremely long flatbed loaded with thick copper pipes. Despite the cold, there were stands on the sidewalks selling late-night snacks: steaming bowls of spicy noodles, bamboo steamers full of baozi, and a man with a brazier of coals selling meat kebobs strung on old bicycle spokes.

"Hey, chiguo fan mei you?" Alex wanted to know if Lu-lu was hungry, and Lu-lu realized she was starving. So they stopped at the noodle stand and each ordered a bowl.

"Wo xihuan la de! Duo fang yi dian lajiao!" Alex urged the surprised man to give her more spice in her bowl.

Lu-lu was impressed with Alex's Beijing consonants, her hard R's at the ends of words and fully enunciated *zh* and *sh* sounds, which were more apparent now that Lu-lu wasn't startled by the American-sounding vowels. Alex was completely at ease chatting with the noodle man and his wife. Lu-lu always preferred to remain as quiet as possible so she could observe the people around her. So long as she didn't speak, she passed for Chinese, something about her round face and the way she held herself made the locals assume Lu-lu was a native, some shy bookish student perhaps. They paid her no mind, which was what she most wanted after the horrors of her adolescence in her small town where she could never blend in. But Alex had no such qualms. She regaled the couple with tales of her life in Beijing.

It was so late after they finished their noodles, that the front gate to the university near Lu-lu's dorm was closed and locked. She had to knock loudly on the small wooden door beside the gate to wake the door guard inside. He was a kind, elderly man, perhaps given this annoying job because he was too old for anything else. He smelled a bit like alcohol, but he was nothing like Lu-lu's mother. He was instead a cheerful drunk, and seeing Lu-lu, his face lit up, recognizing her immediately. He smiled and allowed both Lu-lu and Alex to push their bikes through the small gatehouse and enter the campus without checking or recording Alex's ID.

"Your door guard is cool," Alex remarked in English. Somehow that made Lu-lu feel cooler too, as though it were something she could take credit for—having the foresight to live in such a place instead of just being the beneficiary of dumb luck. It did not occur to Lu-lu that in fact she had been able to cultivate special friendships with people like the door guard. Her quiet kindness had not gone unnoticed.

They walked their bikes through the darkened campus. The electricity was out again. The lights on the windows were all dark, when usually there were always a few bookworms who studied late late late into the night. The city frequently cut power to their block, the better to send power to the late-night construction crews working on office buildings, shopping centers, hotels for foreigners. The students and professors complained, but the city did not care. What were students compared to money?

Sometimes Lu-lu liked to ride alone through the streets of the city, when she felt lonely or sad or some combination of the two. She often returned long after everyone else had gone to sleep. She knew the habits of the dorms, which windows had fresh laundry hanging outside, which had shut down and turned dark early, who studied the longest, even if she didn't know the inhabitants.

"What a beautiful campus," Alex proclaimed. "So charming. So very Chinese."

This made Lu-lu giggle.

"What else would it be?"

"Oh, they're modernizing up in Beijing," Alex said. "All the so-called foreign experts are being put in modern apartment buildings. Grad students too. They're fancy. We have our own kitchens, electricity, heat," she said, "but what's charming about westernization?"

"I don't know. I wouldn't mind a working kitchen and heat," Lu-lu said. "Try living for a winter in Nanjing."

"This is nothing. Beijing is very cold. This feels like fall still."

"It snows here!" Lu-lu insisted. "And there's no heat!"

Alex laughed. "You're so American," she said, and for the first time that evening, Lu-lu felt a little hurt.

But the moment passed because they rounded a corner and all at once the moonlight was flooding through the thicket of trees, blue-white light like a bolt of silk unfolding through the inky campus.

"Zhen piaoliang!" Alex gasped. "Like a Chinese painting."

And Lu-lu had to agree. She felt proud again of her campus.

They paused outside Lu-lu's dormitory. And Lu-lu was not entirely surprised when Alex leaned in and kissed Lu-lu on the cheek, and then on the corner of her mouth. Lu-lu turned toward Alex and kissed her back.

Alex was the one who acted surprised. "I'm a little drunk," she confessed.

"I'm not," Lu-lu said and kissed her again.

Alex ended up staying the night in Lu-lu's dorm. The fuwuyuan who were supposed to be stationed at the front desk by the stairwell, required to take down the ID of anyone who visited, were out. Perhaps the older woman who worked the night shift was using the bathroom down the hall or had stretched out on the cot in the room off the side.

It was easy for Lu-lu and Alex, hand in hand, to run up the stairs, holding in their giggles, unobserved.

"Sit here," Alex said, pointing between her legs, scooting to the very top of the bed, her back against the headboard.

Lu-lu sat against Alex, and Alex held Lu-lu's left breast in her hand, and she placed her fingers between Lu-lu's legs.

"Let me kiss you." Lu-lu tried to turn, tried to hold Alex's beautiful face with her hands, but Alex shook her head. "No, wait," she said.

When Lu-lu orgasmed, she came in a high-pitched cry like a piccolo, which embarrassed her, but Alex squeezed her arms around Lu-lu tightly and allowed Lu-lu to kiss her finally.

They fell asleep together, their arms wrapped around each other.

The next day, when they awoke, the sunlight was spread in a thick buttery slab across their bed. It was late, afternoon already. Alex said, "There's something I should have told you."

"Mm-hm?" Lu-lu said trying not to let her heart breaking show on her face. She knew this could mean only one thing.

Alex explained that she was in a relationship with another foreign student back in Beijing. "But it's an open relationship," she said.

"Mm-hmm," Lu-lu said. She had no idea what anyone meant when someone said this.

"But it's kind of serious," Alex said.

"Mm-hmm."

"I'm sorry," Alex said. "I was a little drunk last night."

You were not that drunk, Lu-lu wanted to say, but she held her tongue. She didn't want to give away her emotions. She didn't want her disappointment to show. She didn't want to cry or do something embarrassing. She felt stupid.

"But I don't have any regrets," Alex said. Alex leaned in close to Lu-lu, pulled her hair away from her face, and kissed her ear.

"Good," said Lu-lu. "I don't either." Then Lu-lu regretted saying that immediately. Why did she have to repeat everything like an idiot parrot?

Then Alex said there was one more thing. She was going back to Beijing in three days.

. . .

After that, Alex never spoke of the open but serious relationship again. Lu-lu showed Alex which bus to take to get to the Sun Yat-sen Mausoleum on Purple Mountain so she could sightsee while Lu-lu was at work. Then on her day off, Lu-lu took Alex to see the thousand Buddhas carved into Qi Xia Mountain, and finally to walk along the city wall where they could gaze out at the villages in the distance. But nothing quite impressed Alex. "You should see the Great Wall," Alex said. She and her friends had gone to picnic there many times. The Great Wall and the Summer Palace and the Forbidden City.

"You'll have to come to Beijing sometime," Alex said. "Beijing has some really cool clubs. They play really good music."

Lu-lu couldn't help but feel there was a little derision in Alex's voice, as though the parties here didn't play such great music.

. . .

Alex slept in Lu-lu's bed, but they didn't make love again after that first night. Alex let Lu-lu kiss her, and she kissed Lu-lu too, but then she said she was tired and turned away, falling immediately into a deep sleep. Two nights in a row. The third morning she had to get up early to catch her train and barely slept at all, and then she was gone.

■ ■ ■

That should have been the end of it, but after Alex left, she wrote Lu-lu the most beautiful letters. She quoted poetry and song lyrics from cool concerts she'd heard live back in L.A. She made Lu-lu a mixtape of bands that Lu-lu had never heard of (and to be honest didn't much like), but when she showed them to the other Americans in the dorm, they were all impressed, so Lu-lu decided the tape meant Alex missed her.

"Come to Beijing," Alex wrote. "I'll show you around all the cool places."

■ ■ ■

Lu-lu decided to visit Alex in Beijing for the lunar new year holiday when she did not have to teach. She wrote to Alex and said she was coming, and Alex wrote back with directions on how to find her apartment. Lu-lu took the train to Beijing. Because she hadn't planned the trip and had to buy her ticket at the last minute, there were tickets available only for the slow train to Beijing. Because of martial law, however, there were still not as many Chinese traveling as would normally, and Lu-lu was able to secure a berth in a sleeper car. Still, Lu-lu found she couldn't sleep for all twelve hours of the ride. She was nervous, and she imagined various scenarios when she saw Alex again. She imagined going to the Great Wall for a picnic and the Summer Palace and Forbidden City. Lu-lu tried to think of clever things to say, references to history, to the Qing dynasty, to Manchu social protocol that she had studied in college back in the States and that she'd found fascinating. She wished she'd thought to bring one of her old textbooks. She was afraid she'd seem boring compared to all of Alex's cool friends in Beijing. She wanted to hold her own.

At the train station, Lu-lu didn't bother with Alex's directions. She didn't want to get lost, so she splurged and took a cab that dropped her off directly at the gate of Alex's apartment complex.

The security guard there took down Lu-lu's ID number and made her wait while he called Alex's apartment, and that's how Lu-lu discovered these apartments had phones in them. Fancy indeed compared to her dormitory in Nanjing. She was relieved when the guard at last allowed her to enter the compound and helpfully pointed out the way among the two-story buildings where the foreign experts and international graduate students lived.

When Lu-lu found the apartment, she knocked once, twice, and then a white American man opened the door.

"Hey," he said, and smiled so that all his teeth showed, which struck Lu-lu as presumptuous. "You must be Lu-lu," he said. "Am I saying the tones right?" He didn't wait for her to reply before saying, "I'm Kyle, Alex's fiancé." He opened the door, still grinning in that odd Cheshire cat manner, and held out his arm as though she were about to enter a grand palace.

So Lu-lu learned that Kyle was a Ph.D. student from UCLA on a research fellowship in Beijing. She watched him as he talked, staring at his overly straight teeth. He was ordinary looking, not really handsome, not cool looking at all. He was a little bit older, which meant he could be about thirty-five—Lu-lu wasn't quite sure how to tell; somewhere between what Lu-lu thought of as normal student age and professor age—with slightly thinning sandy-brown hair, about the same height as Lu-lu, shorter than Alex. He had perfect teeth and very nice manners, and Lu-lu could not concentrate on a word he was saying even though he talked continuously.

Alex appeared from their kitchen. She was wearing a white apron, and her thick black hair was curled and she was wearing mascara and pinkish lipstick. She put some dishes on a table and curled up on a love seat at the end of the table. Kyle put his arm proprietarily over

Alex's beautiful shoulders and looked at her like she was the most beautiful woman he'd ever seen. As though he never doubted her devotion. Lu-lu suspected that Kyle's family had money.

The apartment was incredibly large and well furnished by the standards of Lu-lu's dorm and the few of her Chinese colleagues' apartments that she'd visited. Alex and Kyle had a large dining room table in another room with traditional Chinese rosewood chairs with intricately carved backs, complete with good-luck bats and fruit and blossoms. They had a cabinet inlaid with mother-of-pearl. They had an embroidery that looked like an authentic late-nineteenth-century Manchu-woman's qipao framed behind glass on the wall.

A few more neighbors dropped by.

They sat around the dining table, Lu-lu and Alex and the fiancé and the neighbors from down the hall—a pair of Germans and a Swedish couple—eating plates of peanuts and watermelon seeds with mugs of cold beer, which Lu-lu pretended to drink but found herself merely gripping and ungripping. She discovered the beautiful rosewood chairs were not that comfortable to sit in. The fiancé told a long, boring anecdote about getting lost in Harbin and how a kindly farmer had let him ride on his ox-driven cart, which he drove through the city streets. "We even stopped at all the stoplights." He told this anecdote as though he'd had an amazing experience. "Can you imagine? The two of us sitting on the cart with all these cars and trucks on either side!"

What was he supposed to do? Lu-lu resisted the urge to roll her eyes. *Ride his ox cart on the sidewalk? Or not stop at the red lights and get hit by a bus?*

Lu-lu felt stupid and awkward and crazy and disappointed, crushingly disappointed, to see that in fact Alex probably hadn't really missed her but was merely bored with the fiancé whom she would clearly never leave. The fiancé with money who loved her like all the other beautiful Chinese things he collected.

"Now you must all try this tea," Kyle said. He brought out a clay teapot and told a long tedious story about how special it was and how he'd learned from a "tea master" in Taiwan how to prepare tea "the proper way." He prattled on about "priming" the clay, which meant he poured a cup of hot water into the pot then dumped it out and then poured another cup in and spun it around and poured it out again. It reminded Lu-lu of a Montessori preschool class she'd visited once.

"Good thing we're not very thirsty," Lu-lu said.

To her surprise, Alex chuckled.

Kyle seemed nonplussed and stopped his water-pouring ritual. He brought out a wooden box and announced, "This is a very special tea. From Yunnan. I bought it from a very elderly tea master who swears it has hallucinogenic properties."

"You know a lot of old tea masters," Lu-lu remarked. This time the Swedes laughed as well.

Kyle flushed. He said not to interrupt him while he was finishing the "ritual." It was very important that everything be done properly to bring out the true essence of the tea, which had been very expensive. He even had a special, polished, wooden, flat tea spoon. He scooped out some of the leaves and dropped them into his clay teapot, then commenced with more water pouring. He swirled the water around the pot while holding the teapot with both hands. This "ritual" went on for some time, and then finally he poured everyone a cup of tea.

One taste, and Lu-lu knew poor Kyle had been cheated. The tea was not only bitter, but it also tasted gritty, like dirt. The leaves were old and had broken in the hot water rather than blooming.

One of the Germans drank too quickly and started coughing. His face flushed red, first his nose, then his cheeks, as his cough deepened into a wheeze like a donkey's bray.

"Maybe you can pour him a cup of plain water?" Lu-lu asked.

Kyle's face tightened, a quick tensing of the muscles around his eyes, a flattening of his lips before he could hide his anger behind his bland host's expression.

Lu-lu could imagine the man Kyle would become in twenty, even thirty years, very similar to the man he was now, already an old man destined to grow even older rapidly, his personality hardening into rigidity. A man with a temper. A man who liked things to be exactly one certain way: his way. Lu-lu's heart skipped a beat in her chest, but then she calmed herself. She wasn't the one marrying Kyle. She wouldn't have to be the one suffering under his fastidiousness.

In fact, Lu-lu realized, she needn't suffer a minute more.

"You know, I should head out. It's getting late," Lu-lu said. Her voice was louder than she intended, or maybe she merely thought it sounded louder because she was nervous. Lu-lu didn't like to make people unhappy. It reminded her of making her mother unhappy, but of course everything had made her mother unhappy, no matter what she did. At any rate, Lu-lu couldn't sit here like this anymore, listening to Kyle and his ancient tea master schtick.

The German man was still coughing although not as loudly. His partner thumped him on the back.

"Are you okay?" she asked.

"It's. Just. A. Tickle," he gasped. "In. My. Throat."

Lu-lu fished around in her backpack. "Here. I always travel with this cough syrup. Ever since I got sick at Huang Shan over the National Day break."

She handed the German man one of the vials. "It's really effective traditional medicine. It's made with snake bile, but it tastes like Coca-Cola syrup."

The German man waved his thanks with one hand, as his back curved like a comma. He coughed into his fist.

"I better go," Lu-lu said. "It's late." She was repeating herself. Lu-lu hated when she said awkward things awkwardly. But really, who cared? What did it matter what she said *now*? Was there anything more awkward and stupid than what she'd already done? Hopping on the first train—the slow train to boot—to see Alex. As though Alex would be happy to see her. Lu-lu shuddered.

She stood up. With horror, she thought she might cry. Her vision was already blurring from tears rushing to her eyes. Her nose was burning. Oh no oh no oh no. She could not cry in front of Alex in front of Kyle in front of Alex. She would die. Just die.

Lu-lu slung her backpack's straps over her shoulders. She careened toward the front door. She hoped it was the front door. She found her shoes.

"Wait, where are you going? You're leaving so soon!" Alex's voice wailed from behind.

"Sorry, but I told some friends I was meeting them. It's late. I lost track of the time." Lu-lu cringed inside. She couldn't even lie properly.

Lu-lu slipped her feet into her shoes, and then she was stomping down the hall, shuffling toward the stairwell. She hoped she'd escape before she burst into tears, before anyone saw her.

Thankfully, she realized no one was following her.

Out in the fresh air, the cold slapped her hard against her cheeks. Her skin burned. Lu-lu no longer felt the urge to cry. Alex had been right about one thing. It was colder in Beijing. Nanjing's cold, humid and damp as it was, was nothing like Beijing's arctic vise.

Her lungs hurt, like needles pricking her from the inside with each breath.

She stumbled out of the compound and down the alleyway. She tried to remember the direction the taxi had driven.

It was dark, one street lamp at the corner casting a puddle of yellow light on the asphalt. There were no cabs here so far from the train station.

Oh, another foolish mistake. She should have called a cab from the apartment. They had a phone even!

But no, there was no going back. She marched onward.

Lu-lu was halfway to the main street when the visions hit.

The lamp turned into a sun, its beams radiating into the night sky like lava from a volcano. She could feel the warmth from her position still half a block away. Lu-lu stood still as she watched the sunbeams pour down the lamp onto the inky asphalt, flowing along the dark sidewalk, parting the shadows like a sea, the warm yellow light coming closer and closer. And then Lu-lu saw her, her grandmother. Nai-nai had died when Lu-lu was eight, but now she stood before Lu-lu in the thick padded cotton qipao that she'd had made in Taiwan before she immigrated to the U.S. Nai-nai wasn't smiling (she'd never been that type of grandmother), but she stared straight at Lu-lu, her black eyes bright and intelligent as ever. Nai-nai opened her mouth as though to speak, but Lu-lu couldn't hear.

When Lu-lu was a little girl, before her family moved away from New Jersey to another state far away, to the terrible small town that Lu-lu hated, her grandparents used to babysit while her parents worked or worked out their differences. During those summers, Nai-nai on occasion would leave Lu-lu's grandfather, packing her bags— not in formal luggage but in the plastic shopping bags saved from Chinatown forays—with the provisions for their trip: cough drops, snacks, a thermos of hot tea, and always oranges. Once Nai-nai and Lu-lu made it as far as JFK.

Lu-lu remembered they sat side by side on the plastic molded seats at the gate for international flights, Nai-nai patiently peeling the oranges, then handing one section to Lu-lu, one for herself. They sat and watched families reuniting, pushing carts of luggage piled with boxes tied together with string and tape, Lu-lu and Nai-nai taking turns spitting orange seeds into the plastic bag that Nai-nai had brought along just for this purpose, until Ye-ye figured out the clues she'd left behind and tracked them down.

Lu-lu rested her head on her grandmother's soft shoulder, their bodies melting into each other, drowsing, when she felt an electric current race through Nai-nai's body. Lu-lu woke up, her skin still tingling as though she'd shocked herself, and there he was. Ye-ye. Standing in his gray overcoat, leaning on his cane, his felt hat tilted at an angle on his head—his traveling clothes. He reached out his hand to Nai-nai.

"Let's go home," Nai-nai said. Hui jia qu le. She smiled.

"What was that shock?" Lu-lu asked.

Lu-lu looked around her, at the people sitting on the surrounding seats, some of them staring into space or inspecting their bags or engrossed in conversation.

"Did you feel it, Nai-nai?" Lu-lu's skin still tingled. The hairs in her nostrils vibrated. She could swear they were singed. She could smell the faint whiff of smoke.

But Nai-nai only smiled and pulled Lu-lu up from the chair. Ye-ye walked over and grabbed hold of the plastic bags with the hand that wasn't holding the cane. Nai-nai hooked her arm through his, and then she took Lu-lu's hand and they walked linked together like that back to the bus stop.

The air smelled like that now.

Like ozone, like a wire burning, like the electrons in a lightning bolt.

Like sparks. Like love.

Lu-lu blinked, and her grandmother's ghost was gone. It was snowing. Large flakes fell from black sky. The world was fracturing into a kaleidoscope of black and white dots.

Then she felt the hand on her shoulder. Lu-lu jumped.

"Sorry, sorry, I didn't mean to startle you." It was Alex. She was wearing her green soldier's coat but no hat. The snowflakes settled in her thick black hair like blossoms. Was this real? Was this the tea? But Nai-nai had been real. Lu-lu knew that for certain. Nai-nai had returned just to send her a message in this moment of need. But what exactly was the message?

"I didn't think you'd really come," Alex continued. "I just assumed, I just assumed I'd never see you again."

"But you got my letter. I said I was coming."

"It's so far. And you're busy. You have a job."

Alex's skin glowed golden under the streetlamp, her black eyes wet and bright.

Lu-lu knew she should play it cool. She'd already been humiliated enough. Alex felt sorry for her. That's why she ran out, following her like this; it was pity. Why else? She had that rich boyfriend. Their fancy apartment. His fancy apartment. Lu-lu was poor, and she didn't even know if Alex considered her a girlfriend, or what, or something else. A weekend experiment maybe.

Lu-lu swallowed. She could smell orange blossoms.

"I wanted to see you again," Lu-lu said. What did she have to lose? She closed her eyes, made a wish. "I missed you." There. She said it.

"Really?"

"I missed you every day since you went back to Beijing. All seventeen and a half days."

Alex threw an arm around Lu-lu's shoulders and pulled her face close to hers and kissed her. Their noses bumped, and Lu-lu's glasses pressed up against the bridge of her nose, but she didn't care, she held onto Alex tight and kissed her soft lips, touched her soft tongue with hers. They were on the street and anyone could see them, and she didn't care.

Lightning flashed, and then there was a rumble of thunder, like mountains of rocks breaking apart and crashing together again, elemental.

■ ■ ■

Alex and Lu-lu returned to Nanjing together that night. Lu-lu assured Alex there was no need for her things. They could buy anything she needed in Nanjing. There were no sleeper berths available, only hard seats, and only the slowest train, not the direct one, so they'd stop at every village en route to Nanjing, an eighteen-hour-and-twenty-six-minute trip. Farmers boarded bearing three or four striped plastic bags each, their gifts for their families now that the season of the lunar holiday rush home had arrived; martial law be damned, people wanted to return to their villages to see their families. Alex and Lu-lu sat side by side, arm in arm, leaning against each other for the warmth.

A man in a thick padded coat and padded pants that made him look three times his natural size made his way down the aisle, opening a plastic bag for other passengers to peruse, offering roast ducks for purchase. A woman seated across the table offered them flavored watermelon seeds. Another man peeled a bright red apple with a knife, the long peel curling unbroken like a snake coiling.

Lu-lu silenced the little voice in her head that liked to criticize her every move and second-guess her every thought. She allowed herself to be bathed in the feeling of being loved. It didn't matter anymore that the feeling might not last, at least not as long as she had thought she wanted. In fact, these feelings might change as the hours on the train wore on, when Alex's competitive streak began to get on Lu-lu's nerves, when Lu-lu's tendency to self-doubt dimmed and her growing awareness of her own self-worth increased, but that might be hours and hours and hours away.

Right now, Lu-lu understood, this moment was enough. She'd gone to Beijing and wooed Alex back. She'd proven there were some Chinese things that could not be bought but had to be earned.

The Nanny

·····

The woman closed the satellite phone and set it in her purse, a large shiny leather bag that opened and shut with an expensive sounding *CLICK*. Killing animals for their skins had been banned for decades as a waste of resources, but the purse looked new and it didn't look synthetic. Anping wondered what kind of bribes were paid and to whom for such a bag to exist and what kind of wealthy people the woman must work for even to want to carry such an item.

"Ayi, let me introduce myself. My name is Xu Wen. I work for the employment agency." She handed Anping a card. It held a hologram of Miss Xu Wen in even more makeup than she was wearing now, smiling with all her teeth showing.

Squinting, Anping tried to make out the characters on the card. She'd had a full elementary school education, but there hadn't been much need for her to read with the exception of the subtitles on the soap operas she enjoyed when the young people used new terms she was unfamiliar with. The card said something about the *Heaven's Blessing Auntie Service. Serving all your domestic needs*. The pod car hit an air pocket, the card flew out of Anping's hand, and the driver swore, then apologized.

"They told me you understand about modern living and all that?"

"Modern living?"

The woman blew her breath over her teeth. "You know, how to monitor water flow levels and how to report irregularities. How to compost. How to program the kitchen stove. You were assigned to terrarium planting duty, but I was told you know how to use colony appliances? There were communal kitchens in your dormitory?"

"My husband and I had married worker housing until he had to return to Earth. I monitored all the housing systems myself."

"Good, good, good. I'm delighted to hear this! Not all farm colony workers have such a good background. So you are familiar with the technology. That's the main thing. They told me you wouldn't need much training."

"Excuse me, Miss Xu—"

"Call me Sally. Everyone does."

"Sha Lei?" Anping repeated the sounds uncertainly when the driver hit another air hole, braked suddenly, and three young men on fancy personal jetpacks took the opportunity to dart in front of the pod car, each one reaching out to smack the hood with a gloved fist, one after the other.

"Little bastards," the driver hissed.

"Watch your tongue in front of Ayi."

"Sha Lei, I don't understand. What kind of training? What kind of job am I going to have?"

The toothy Sally shook her head so that her large gold earrings seemed in danger of flying off her head. "Ayi, you are very, very lucky. I have found a wonderful position for you. Working for a very kind lady. You're going to be living in a very fancy apartment. One of the best in New Shanghai Colony. Really, it's a very fortunate job for you, coming from a terrarium unit and all. You're a little older than I usually work with to be honest, but I can see you're very refined for a farming colony woman. And luck was in your favor. This client needed someone immediately. Everyone else quit. So superstitious, some of these girls."

Anping almost asked what the pretentious Sha Lei meant but held her tongue. Working for a rich woman in a fancy apartment offered some advantages. For one, the rich woman would certainly have a better satellite phone than Anping's. There had been a solar storm, and her signal wasn't strong enough to reach her grandson back on Earth in Original China. The other advantage, of course, was the higher salary.

Anping could not keep track of the number of streets they passed as they left the neighborhood of the portal where migrants from the various colonies could catch transportation to and from their new work assignments. Anping and her husband had arrived three years ago to work on Henan II Farm Colony 17. They'd agreed to a three-year contract to pay off the mortgage that they'd taken out on their Earth hukou in order to pay off their son's debts. He'd run into some business problems, but he was a hardworking and capable man, and Anping knew that he'd be able to get on his feet again. But then things had gone from bad to worse in his business, he and his wife had had to take on a long-term shipping contract to a mining colony on one of Jupiter's moons, and her grandson had technically inherited his parents' debt. Then Anping's husband had a heart attack and needed to go back to Earth early. Anping had agreed to take on his labor contract so that authorities would release him. Technically, she now had four more years to go before she could pay off her mortgage.

Anping thought it was a good sign that her grandson had found steady work on a cloud-seeding station above their village. The first year he'd called her almost every month, always a new complaint. He was lonely. His business partners were blaming him for all their mistakes. At that rate, Anping had despaired of her grandson ever saving enough money to marry. But now things were at last looking up.

When the labor recruiter had come to the farm colony to see if any of the women had wanted to work in New Shanghai, she'd jumped at the chance.

"Don't go to the city," one of the other women had cautioned. "They work you night and day. At least here we have our own dormitory. If you live with your boss, you never rest."

But Anping wanted the extra money.

. . .

Finally, the pod car took an exit, and they whooshed toward a residential complex.

"You see, first-class apartment building," Sally pointed to the imposing metal gate. A camera followed their movements. "It's me," Sally spoke into a metal box. Anping looked at the metal box and saw a small screen with her own face peering over Sally's shoulder.

A man's voice commanded, "ID!"

Sally dug around in her enormous handbag, flashed a card from her wallet at the camera, then *CLICK*, shut the bag again.

"Enter!" the man's metallic voice again.

The doors of the green metal gate slid apart.

"You see, very safe. No riffraff can get in here."

"What if the people inside want to get out? Then what do we do?"

Sally laughed but didn't answer.

The pod car descended to ground level. The doors slid open, and Anping gasped despite herself. But the air inside the dome was fit for humans, and Sally hopped out. Anping followed her cautiously.

"This is the courtyard, very nice, very safe. You can let the child run around here. Hmm. Nice fountain. That's new." Sally nodded at the sculpture of two giant koi fish in bronze with massive spouts of liquid shooting from their gaping mouths.

"Is that real water?" Anping gasped.

"No, no, of course not. It's just an illusion." Sally squinted at the array of round doorways. "And here's your building. Number 828-188. They all look alike. That was a design mistake if you ask me. Try to remember the location. The numbers are all very similar too. These rich people are very superstitious. Eight this, eight that. But don't say I said that."

Anping tried to find a way to remember the number, repeating it in her head.

Sally tapped impatiently at a button on the wall. She had long red fingernails. Anping wondered how she washed dishes or chopped vegetables with such long nails. She imagined one of the nails breaking, embedded in a cucumber.

The metal doors to one building slid open as Sally extended an arm, gesturing for Anping to enter. Anping squared her shoulders, took a deep breath, and entered, but no, it was not the apartment; it was a small windowless room. Sally grabbed hold of the bar on the wall and gestured for Anping to follow suit. She felt a slight shudder, and then the door opened again.

"We're here!" Sally said brightly.

Sally led her down the relatively plain hallway. The walls were painted in two colors, white on top, pale green below. The carpet was thin and stained in places. "Not so fancy here," Sally noted. She kicked at a stain on the carpet with the toe of her shiny high-heeled shoe. "Someone put his cigarette out on the carpet. Some people! All money, no culture." She laughed.

Yes, thought Anping. *Some people!*

At the end of the hall, Sally let Anping into the apartment where she was to work and live as a nanny. It was dimly lit. Anping blinked, trying to see clearly.

"The client needs to keep the lights low. Too much light hurts her eyes." Sally shrugged. She opened a few doors and peered inside, the closet, a cabinet, the bedroom. She took stock of the furniture of the mysterious woman whom Anping would be working for. Anping felt uncomfortable as Sally marched about, looking into the woman's closet, pulling out a checkered blazer, then a blouse, checking for labels.

Anping put her bag down beside her feet and held very still. She felt dizzy. She could tell even though the curtains were drawn that the apartment was very high in the air. It was almost as though she could feel the building swaying in the wind, which she knew was impossible. The winds blew outside the domes. Should the wind ever enter the biospheres, the least of anyone's worries would be the buildings' swaying. The oxygen would be sucked out. The gravitational generators could explode. And everyone who could not get to the underground safety tunnels would be dead.

Back in the early days of the Mars colony, there had been accidents. Meteorites had crashed into a dome, and the colonists had all perished. Or perhaps it had been a terrorist attack from a rival colony. The news was never transparent on these disasters. But that had been decades ago. Long before Anping had arrived. She assumed the government had figured out the technology to protect against meteorites, or terrorists.

"Here's your room." Sally opened a door and pointed to the narrow bed, the spare dresser. "Not bad. I've seen worse. And here's the kitchen." She pointed behind Anping, who refused to turn.

"Well, you must be tired. I should let you get settled in."

"But where is the woman?"

"The client will be home soon, I'm sure. You can just wait in your room or sit there on the sofa. I don't think anyone would mind if you get yourself a drink of hot water, but don't touch the refrigerator until the client shows you. These types are always particular like that." Sally clicked-clacked across the kitchen in her heels. Anping heard the refrigerator door swish open, then shut. "Good. It's full."

Anping tried not to look at all the furniture, all the vases and paintings and tall lamps and shiny things, every corner jammed with something. All these *things* made her dizzy. Even though she knew it was not possible, she felt the floor swaying, all the sharp shiny *things* on the verge of tipping to the floor.

Her glance fell on a picture on the wall, amid the garish renditions of the Great Wall and the Qin emperor's terra-cotta warriors and a pair of kittens nuzzling. On the central screen was a simple family photograph, similar to the one Anping had had on her own wall at home on Earth. It showed a man, a woman (her new boss, she assumed), and a little girl in pigtails. Anping was relieved the child was not a baby but instead looked to be about three or four years old. Babies were endlessly needy, but a child could be reasoned with. Or bribed.

Anping approached the wall and looked into the woman's face. Was she kind? Foolish? Demanding? But she looked like any beautiful young woman in a picture these days, her features rendered perfect and bland by the camera filter or some kind of surgery, her hair sprayed perfectly in place, her smile frozen on her face.

"Well, now that you're familiar with the place, I'll be leaving. I've got more work to attend to. You've got my card if you need me. Just give me a call on my cell." Sally was halfway down the hall when she called back to Anping, her finger pressed to the implant in her ear. Then she was talking to someone else, "Wei? . . . It's me again. Yes, as usual . . . I'm coming. If the traffic isn't—" Sally waved goodbye and was gone, the door clicking shut behind her. Then the door opened again suddenly. "Don't wander about in the hallway. These doors lock automatically, and your prints haven't been entered into the system yet!" Then the door closed again and Sally was gone.

Anping picked up her luggage and went to the tiny room off the kitchen that Sally said was to be hers. There was a bright quilt on top of the bed; a small, square window that could be programmed to show scenes of Original China or of the solar system; a dresser. She sat on the edge of the bed and discovered it was too soft. Anping sighed dejectedly. Then she noticed the mirror on the wall. It faced the bed—bad feng shui; she'd have to change it or hang a towel atop before she slept at night. Otherwise the reflection would spread unlucky qi upon her body and she would grow ill. The young were foolish and didn't believe anymore, but Anping was not about to take any chances.

Anping stood up and examined herself. Her reflection surprised her, this old woman staring back. Anping hadn't realized until now just how she'd aged. Her face lined, her hair short and gray and wiry. Her worrying about her son's financial troubles had taken its toll. She turned her face left then right, looking for a better, less alarming angle.

Or perhaps she'd always looked like this, looked like this for years and years and just never known. This is what an old woman who'd worked her entire life in the countryside looked like. This is what the girls who had left Earth to work in the colonies were afraid of becoming.

Anping turned away from the mirror.

She inspected her room instead. The dresser was small but clean. She was wondering if she should unpack now or wait till her employer arrived when the satellite phone slid out of a hole in the pocket of her jacket where she had tucked it for safekeeping. It was her most expensive possession, and her son had given it to her before she had blasted off to the colony. Most farm workers had had to queue up at the station to call family at home, but she'd had her very own phone, although the high cost of calls meant she had to save scrupulously, eschewing any of the expensive holo-films or karaoke bars, and certainly the virtual majong parlors, in order to afford to use it.

She knelt down on her hands and knees atop the bright throw rug meant to mimic an embroidery of butterflies and peonies and peered under the bed to see if the phone might have rolled there when she felt a drop of liquid fall on her hand. Then another. To her surprise, she saw a drop of red blossom into a rose petal on the rug. Her nose was bleeding. The air in the apartment was too dry.

She sat up quickly, pressing her nostrils shut with one hand and tilting her head back while she hunted in her purse for a handkerchief or tissue, but she had nothing.

Her head still tilted back, Anping wandered down the metallic hallway—she'd known all the sharp edges were bad luck!—and found her way back to the kitchen. Surely there had to be a dishrag, a cloth, something. She squeezed her nostrils with one hand and pulled drawers open with the other. Cutlery. Western-style forks and knives and spoons, a whole drawer full. Then another drawer containing nothing but knives. Another with strange objects for cooking that Anping did not recognize. Who were these people? Who lived like this?

She searched under the sink, tilting her head to the side as best she could to see if there might be a dishrag there, but there was only a metal compactor. She tried the upper cabinets. Plates, bowls, a wok, finally an empty barbecue sauce jar with chopsticks sticking out. Another cabinet of food in boxes. Ridiculous! Who ate so little?

Finally, in desperation she tried the giant two-door refrigerator. If she could just get something cold to press against her nose.

Anping was rummaging through the freezer, shocked at the sheer number of packages of premade food—fried baby squid, fish in bean sauce, fully formed baozi, curries frozen into brown ice puddles— when the front door opened with a swoosh.

"Careful, careful," a woman's voice admonished. "Hua Hua, what did I tell you? Don't shove."

Anping closed the freezer door quickly and turned just in time to find a little girl of about four standing in the doorway staring at her. Anping tried to smile at the child without letting go of her nostrils. She managed a grimace.

"Mama!" the girl cried.

The sound of heels clicking. A woman, very well dressed, extremely thin, and wearing quite a lot of makeup appeared in the doorway. She looked Anping up and down.

"Who. Are. You?"

"I'm the new maid."

"Maid? I didn't order a—oh, you're the nanny for Hua Hua. You're not the maid. We already have a self-cleaning program."

"The woman"—Anping tried but couldn't remember the crazy name—"she didn't tell me much."

"And she left you here all alone? You're bleeding. Here, let me get you something." The woman tap-tap-tapped over to one of the myriad cabinet doors and pulled out a box of tissues and a roll of cleaning towels. She pulled a handful of tissues from the box, rolled them expertly into paper tusks, ran them under the cold tap, and handed them to Anping, who gratefully plugged one up her left nostril. The woman handed her a towel. "For your hands."

"You're all bloody," the little girl said, giggling. "You got blood on everything."

"Hua Hua, be polite to Ayi."

"I wasn't trying to steal your food," Anping said quickly.

The woman now folded her arms and gave Anping an appraising eye. "Did Sally explain the situation here?"

Sally. That was it. "No." Anping pulled one of her tissue tusks out and replaced it with a clean one. She wished she hadn't been caught in such an undignified state. It was inauspicious.

"I should have known. All right, your duties are to take care of Hua Hua. She's a good girl. She won't give you much trouble. She goes to the local you'er yuan in this compound. It's not far from the building. Five minutes' walk. She goes in at nine and is finished by two. You need to prepare a snack for her to take with her for midday and then fix her another snack after you pick her up in the afternoon. Her snacks are in the freezer. She has many allergies and can only eat these packets prepared for her diet. You must never eat them yourself. I will give you as much food as you need, but Hua Hua's meals are special. She has a schedule of activities every day. I suppose Sally didn't give you the list either? I didn't think so. I'll print one out for you tonight. You can read, can't you?"

"Yes. Of course." Anping assumed the list could not be too complicated.

"Good. That's what I asked for. All the lessons are in the compound. You'll have to pick her up and bring her back. Some nights if I'm having a rough time, you'll need to make her dinner as well. You must keep your food separate from Hua Hua's. One mistake could be fatal. To you both. On my treatment days, I won't come home and you'll have to stay in Hua Hua's room. She's afraid of the dark. If you tell her a story, she'll fall asleep. Or let her watch a children's program. If things get very bad, I have the numbers of the doctors you can call."

"I'm sorry, Miss. I don't understand. What things would get bad? Why would I need to call a doctor?"

The woman swore. "Sally really didn't tell you anything, did she? No wonder she ran out of here so quickly. Well, if you want to quit, you can. It's your choice after all. I'm not about to keep you prisoner. I'm sick. I have the blood cancer. Does that bother you?"

Anping shook her head. She'd heard of the condition. Something to do with the radiation on the colony. Some people couldn't handle it. Anping had been lucky. She'd adapted to life on Mars with surprising ease. After the initial nausea from the rocket journey over and a few months of vertigo from the weaker gravity, with the meds prescribed by the colony medical team, she'd been fine.

"Some of the previous nannies were not so sure. They think it's bad luck."

"At least it's not contagious." Anping realized her words sounded insensitive, but the woman laughed.

"Yes, good way to think of it."

"And when your husband comes home from work?" Anping asked. "Should I make dinner for him too, when you . . . when you are having your treatments?"

"I'm not married. Hua Hua's father won't be coming here for a while. He's visiting his wife back in New Taiwan Industrial Colony. I can see Sally didn't tell you about that either. Does *that* bother you?"

Heavens, thought Anping, *am I living in a concubine villa?* She'd heard of the fancy apartment compounds paid for by foreign businessmen, mainly when they were denounced on the news back home. Such selfish men. Monopolizing women. The policies of selfish men over a hundred years ago had led to the shortage of women, and now rich men dared to hoard. How would her grandson ever compete with these scoundrels? But Anping was in no position to complain. The salary was more than double what she'd make on the farm colony.

Hua Hua returned with a bucket filled with ice crystals. "Ayi, here's your ice."

"Thank you, Hua Hua. What a good girl you are!" the woman said. "You must have been looking in your Baba's bar!"

"I'm not a good girl," Hua Hua announced. "I'm a little monkey!" She ran from the kitchen.

Anping held the ice bucket in her hands. Her nose had stopped bleeding by now, but she didn't know where to put it.

"Could you tell I was sick when you saw me?" the woman asked suddenly.

"Oh, no. You look beautiful. Like a movie star," Anping answered truthfully. She was startled by the young woman's beauty, in fact. The photo in the living room was not the result of camera filters. The woman really looked like this.

"Hmm." The woman pursed her lips. "I wanted to be a model once. I used to practice drawing on my face in front of a mirror. I could imitate all the top models, all the actresses. But that was a long time ago. Back in my village."

"You're from a village?"

"Oh, yes. But I left for the city as soon as I had a chance."

The woman took the bucket out of Anping's hands and dumped the ice into the sink into the RECYCLE side. The water would be purified and reused. Still, it struck Anping as cavalier the way the woman and her daughter used so much water. Back on Earth in Anping's village, it hadn't rained naturally for four years before she left. So much of their daily life had been consumed with saving water, maintaining the water recycling facilities, maintaining the cloud-seeding drones.

"I'll let you get acquainted with Hua Hua," the woman said cheerfully. "Let her show you her toys. That will keep her busy. I'll prepare dinner tonight."

Anping nodded as she tried to absorb her new situation. She headed toward the child's bedroom door then turned. "Oh, Miss, what should I call you?"

"How funny. We've done everything backward. My surname is Gao. My name is Ling. You can me Xiao Ling," she said warmly.

"Wu Anping." Anping pointed to her own nose.

"Wu Ayi." Xiao Ling nodded. "Welcome to our home. I hope you'll be very comfortable here."

Anping nodded in thanks. At least the woman didn't put on airs.

. . .

As the weeks passed in her new position, Anping was pleased to discover that her new job was not as onerous as working on the farm colony and her new boss was mostly pleasant, entertaining in fact.

At night, Xiao Ling liked to impersonate her favorite stars. Sometimes in the middle of a soap opera, Xiao Ling would jump up from the sofa and re-enact the scene they'd just watched, playing all the roles herself. Hua Hua was thrilled. She clapped her hands and followed her mother, mimicking her gestures. Sometimes she tried a few lines herself; sometimes she merely ran in circles around her mother, excited to be part of the play even if she didn't understand the plot.

Anping loved the soaps and the beautiful gigantic color screen that projected the holographic images so that Anping felt she herself sat with the nineteenth-century courtiers and consorts depicted. At first Xiao Ling's antics annoyed her, as they inevitably disrupted the show, but she laughed along anyway.

"You've missed your calling! You should have been an actress!" Anping said. "You're prettier than the girl on TV."

"Mama is the most pretty girl in the whole colony," Hua Hua said.

Xiao Ling laughed. "No. Hua Hua is the prettiest girl in the whole universe." Xiao Ling unknotted the flowered silk scarf she wore around her neck and placed it over Hua Hua's black hair, found her radiation glasses on the end table and put them on her daughter. "Look at our movie star!" Taking her cue, Hua Hua sashayed around the living room, hands on her hips, peering over her shoulder, the sunglasses sliding down her nose.

Young girls learn fast these days, Anping thought, even as she laughed along.

"Maybe Hua Hua will have better luck than her mother." Xiao Ling patted at her tousled hair. She sat back down on the sofa, her cheeks flushed. "How could a girl like me become a movie star? No one looks for girls to join the Central Academy for Dramatic Arts in a village. Isn't that right, Ayi?"

She didn't wait for an answer. Xiao Ling was restless, in one of her moods. Anping had been studying Xiao Ling, trying to learn to read her. Everything depended upon this relationship. If Anping pleased her new boss, she'd be able to pay her mortgage twice as fast as she would working on the terrarium unit.

Xiao Ling went to the bar. "Want a drink, Ayi?"

"Oh, no. I'm too old."

"Don't be silly. What's this 'too old' business? How about a scotch?"

"What's that? Foreign wine?"

"You're right. Why should we drink foreigner's wine? We Chinese can make our own wine. How about a beer?" She pulled out two bottles of Colony Pijiu.

"I can't drink a full bottle."

Xiao Ling smiled. "At least you're not saying no." Xiao Ling put one glowing bottle back. She popped the cap off expertly on the side of the bar, slipping the bottle under the edge of the countertop and pulling up hard. Bubbles ran down the side of the bottle.

"Here." She handed one to Anping.

"Mama, I want a taste."

"It's not appropriate for your age. How about a Coke? This is just for you." Xiao Ling pulled a bottle marked with Hua Hua's name and poured some of the dark liquid for the girl.

"Here, Ayi! You try some!" Hua Hua held out the glass.

"No, no, no! This is for you, Hua Hua!" Xiao Ling said sharply. "You know you can't share your food."

Hua Hua's face blanched.

"It's okay, I don't like sweet drinks," Anping said. She raised her beer bottle and took another sip. The beer was better than rice wine. It didn't burn. But it would be better with food.

"Are you hungry?" she asked Xiao Ling hopefully. "I can make us a snack."

"No, I'm fine. Don't trouble yourself. Just sit and relax, Ayi. You're not my servant."

Anping sat on the edge of the sofa. Something salty. The rice crackers Hua Hua liked to munch on after class would be just the thing. But of course she wouldn't touch Hua Hua's special food. Everything for her was kept in carefully marked, sealed containers. Anping couldn't help but wonder if there was something unhealthy about living on the colony for children. There hadn't been any children on the farm colony at all.

Xiao Ling had nearly finished her glass of beer.

"Don't look so worried, Ayi. Are you unhappy here?"

"No, no, no. I'm very happy." Anping spoke quickly, but then she was startled. She was in fact happy here. It was very comfortable to live in this big apartment with only the three of them. She didn't have to queue up to use the communal kitchen or the toilets or shower facilities. It was a little lonely as there were no group activities, like majong, but better to save money. "How about a snack? Would Hua Hua like some of her rice crackers?" Anping suggested.

"Yes, crackers!" Hua Hua squealed.

"Absolutely not!" Xiao Ling's voice was sharp. "What did I tell you, Ayi? You must never eat Hua Hua's food. It is very expensive. Her father has it shipped from New Taiwan just for her."

"I didn't mean that I was going to—"

"Ayi, I understand many things might be confusing here," Xiao Ling's voice took on a condescending tone. "But there are reasons for my rules. Do you understand?"

"Yes, I understand. I will never ever eat any of Hua Hua's food. It is just for her. She has many allergies. I remember," Anping said.

Then Hua Hua let out a wail. She'd spilled her Coke on her dress, a pale pink lacy affair with many ruffles and ribbons. "Mama!" Hua Hua's face crumpled, her chin vibrating. Anping had seen this look before, the child on the verge of a crying fit.

Anping picked her up quickly. "Don't worry, Hua Hua. Ayi will clean your dress. It's time for bed now." And Hua Hua quieted down in Anping's arms and allowed herself to be carried to her lovely little bedroom, as quiet and well appointed as any princess's.

The girl was spoiled beyond all reason, Anping knew, but tonight Hua Hua's fragility had spared her from enduring more of Xiao Ling's rage. *What a pain rich city girls are!* Anping thought.

. . .

The next couple of weeks had passed without incident when Anping awoke one night to a sound so strange she wondered what hungry ghost had strayed on the wind and crept into the bedroom. Her mother used to tell her such stories when they slept huddled together in the winter, lying under a pile of quilts on the kang, their earthen bed with the hollow space beneath for warm coals.

Hungry ghosts are lost spirits. Their families have forgotten them.

No one burns paper money at their graves, no one puts rice and sweets out for them to eat, no one bows before stone tablets bearing their names, only weeds grew on their unswept graves. They have lost their way between this world and the next, and thus they travel on the wind. That's the sound of their crying. The rain is their tears, her mother had told her.

When I die, you mustn't forget me, Anping. No matter where you are. You must never forget me because my family won't remember me. My own mother is dead and my father didn't want another girl. I'm a stranger in this village, and no one here keeps the old ways anymore. But when you're an old woman—

When I'm as old as you, Mama?

Older even than me. Don't forget me, Anping. And I'll watch over you. Promise me, Anping.

And her mother cried, tears sliding down her cheeks as they huddled close together, the storm raging outdoors, and Anping wondered what it would be like to be an old woman, older than her mother. She couldn't imagine such a thing when she was a girl, with her father on the far side of the kang snoring, too tired from working in the fields all day to tell stories at night, and the whole world was comprised of the dark space she and her mother inhabited beneath the quilts, her mother's soft voice whispering in her ear.

A wail. Followed by the whimper of a wounded animal.

Anping sat up straight in bed, completely awake this time. There was a night-light on in the hallway. Anping remembered where she was. She was an old woman, living as a nanny in a rich woman's apartment in New Shanghai. Her mother was long dead, and the sound of the hungry ghost was coming from another room. But Anping didn't believe in ghosts anymore.

She slid her feet over the side of the bed and found her slippers on the floor. She padded down the hallway, listening for the whimpering sound. Had an animal found its way inside? City people liked to keep dogs these days, but dogs were dangerous. They hadn't adjusted well to life on the colony. They contracted mysterious illnesses, they bit people in fits, and they spread sickness. Most people could not afford the licenses for such dangerous creatures, and they were outlawed on the farm colony, but she understood that the wealthy lived by different rules. One of their neighbors in the building, in fact, had a dog, a dark, thick-chested beast with a lionlike mane around its head, some kind of designer breed. She'd seen the man walking it in the courtyard at night.

Anping wished she had a weapon. She thought about grabbing the vase from the polished table in the hallway, but even if she used it in self-defense against a mad dog, could she afford to pay for the vase out of her salary?

Perhaps she could sneak up on the animal, lock it in a room or lure it out with food. She might not have to break anything expensive.

Another whimper. Coming from Xiao Ling's room. The bedroom door was closed but not locked. Anping pressed the button, and it opened quickly. Greenish light flooded from a door in the corner that led to Xiao Ling's very own toilet and bath. The bed sheets were rumpled, pillows lay about the floor, but Xiao Ling was not there. She'd had a doctor visit that afternoon, and that evening she'd prepared a foul-smelling herbal brew that made her tired after she drank it. She'd gone to bed early without watching any of their usual soap opera.

Anping held her breath, tried to hear more than the sound of her own heart beating in her ears. She crept inside and snatched up one of the pillows from the carpet. It would make a weapon of sorts. Or at least something for the animal to bite besides Anping. Perhaps the animal had bitten Xiao Ling. Quietly, wishing she weren't wearing such thin, straw slippers, Anping tiptoed toward the open door to the bathroom.

Xiao Ling was lying on the floor, shaking violently.

"Aiya! What's happening?"

Anping rushed toward her. There was vomit on the toilet seat, in the toilet, on the floor. It stank like the herbs that Xiao Ling had drunk earlier.

"We should call a doctor."

"No," Xiao Ling gasped. "I can't go."

Anping flushed the toilet. She snatched up some toilet paper and wiped Xiao Ling's face, then put the satiny pillow beneath Xiao Ling's head.

Anping glanced around the bathroom. The counter around the sink was covered with bottles—perfume, makeup, medicine. Finally, a cup. Anping filled it from the thermos on the counter and brought it to Xiao Ling. "Try to drink some water."

Xiao Ling couldn't lift her own head, so Anping helped her sit up. The younger woman sipped the hot water. Then suddenly she pushed Anping away, and Xiao Ling was vomiting violently into the toilet again. The sound like a hungry ghost's roar echoed tinnily off the tile floor and walls.

After Xiao Ling was finished, she sank back to the floor onto her pillow.

Anping grabbed a towel from the rack on the wall, ran it under the tap to wash Xiao Ling's face.

"Bring me my medicine," Xiao Ling whispered.

"Your herbs?"

"No. The medicine by my bed. On the nightstand."

Anping found a yellow bottle. She squinted at the characters on the side and her stomach dropped. Xiao Ling was taking neo-plasma, a medicine for clones. Suddenly everything became clear. Why the other nannies had quit. What self-respecting original human would work as a servant to a clone?

Her heart in her throat, Anping held onto the end table. She felt as she had when she'd first moved in, the sensation that the floor was tipping to one side.

Anping hadn't realized a clone could look so natural. The clones she'd seen on the news had always looked visibly off. Their voice was not quite in sync with their facial expressions. They moved as if on slight delay. But Xiao Ling was perfect. She seemed like an original human.

Anping felt a kind of fury burning through her chest. How could she have missed the signs? Or perhaps there were no longer any signs? She wondered if that terrible sneaky Sally was laughing, wherever she was, thinking how she'd fooled Anping, such a bumpkin. But then Anping calmed herself. She counted as she inhaled, counted slowly as she exhaled, until her heart no longer thudded in her chest like a shoe thrown down a flight of stairs.

She knew it would do no good to get angry now. Anping hadn't been paid yet, and she did not need to remind herself that she needed the money. She'd mortgaged her hukou birth certificate that allowed her to live on Earth so that she could afford the trip to the colony because the salaries here were so much higher than anything she could earn on Earth. Her husband and grandson were dependent on her to earn enough money to pay off her grandson's debts so that he could marry or they'd never have a grandchild. The family would die out.

Anping brought the bottle back to Xiao Ling. She poured a few drops into the cup of water, and Xiao Ling clutched the cup with both hands, gulping the liquid noisily.

Xiao Ling clutched her stomach, and Anping thought she might be sick again, but this time Xiao Ling merely panted a bit, then lay back, still.

"I know what you're thinking," Xiao Ling said at last, her voice thick from the drug.

"How can you know what I'm thinking? I'm an original human. You have no idea what our thoughts are like."

"But I do," Xiao Ling said. "I have all the memories of my original. I understand her thoughts. Her feelings are my feelings."

"You mimic her feelings. You really are a great actress!"

"No, they're real," Xiao Ling insisted. "They're my real feelings." She started crying, tears bubbling from her eyes, snot pooling under her nose.

"Oh, all right, they're your real feelings," said Anping, taking pity on her.

"You believe me, don't you? Don't you believe me, Ayi?"

"I can see you and your feelings right now."

Xiao Ling grabbed hold of Anping's hand and clutched it. Anping patted the clone's head as she might a small child's. Eventually Xiao Ling calmed and stopped crying. Anping helped her to get up off the bathroom floor and go back to her bed. Anping tucked the clone's sheets around her body.

"Thank you, Ayi," the clone sighed. Eventually the clone fell asleep.

Anping stood beside the bed, watching Xiao Ling's thin, still body. Anping marveled that she looked so very, very much like an original. "Don't worry," Anping whispered at last. "I believe you."

• • •

Lying in her bed, Anping could not sleep. Her mind raced.

She hadn't realized a clone could actually give birth. The technology must have improved. She had grown so fond of the two of them, both Xiao Ling and Hua Hua. *It would have been nice to have had a daughter*, Anping realized. Someone to dress in pretty clothing from time to time. A girl to help with the chores. Someone to confide in.

Anping allowed herself to imagine bringing Hua Hua to Earth to her village if Xiao Ling couldn't get better. The Taiwanese man was back with his wife. He undoubtedly had other children or he wouldn't have left this one so long. What if Anping and her husband offered to adopt the girl and raise her as their own? She would grow beautiful like her mother. She was smart, doing well in school. When she was old enough, they'd be able to attract a wealthy spouse for her, or perhaps she'd be able to attend a good university, find a career to support herself, and have many choices. They wouldn't mention the mother was a clone. No one need know in their village. Hua Hua would be known only as the orphaned daughter of unfortunate colonists who'd succumbed to the harsh conditions on Mars.

She'd just have to convince Xiao Ling. But what could Anping offer her?

She turned over in her bed, staring at the virtual images of Original China running in the window, a series of landscapes, historic mountains, lakes with lotus, pristine bamboo forests. Anping's village looked like none of these famous places, yet there were times Anping missed it terribly: the crispness of the air on a fall morning, the smell of jasmine blossoms on the night breeze, the sounds in the wind, the way she knew all her neighbors and their children and their parents and grandparents, the pleasure of gossiping around a table while making dumplings for the new year. There was nothing comparable to this in New Shanghai. The village could not compete with the luxury of the apartment and its many conveniences, but natural air and the sensations of living on Earth, these were things the colony would never know.

Then she thought of another scenario. Why wait to see if Xiao Ling died? Why not bring her back too? Maybe she would get better on Earth? A clone wasn't an ideal wife by traditional standards, but Xiao Ling would make a pretty good daughter-in-law, and she already had a child. Who was to say a family couldn't be chosen this way?

. . .

The next day Anping decided to tell Xiao Ling her plan while Hua Hua was at school.

Xiao Ling had stayed at home and was resting in her room when Anping tapped on the door to check on her. Anping sat on the foot of her bed, watching Xiao Ling's pale face, her black hair spread out in waves across her pillows.

Anping took a breath and began before she lost her nerve. "Come back to Earth with me. You could marry my grandson. He won't know you're a clone, and I'll never tell him. You can be an original on Earth. No one would know about your life here."

Xiao Ling did not seem as shocked as Anping had worried. "What would I do? How would I make a living if I left my lao gong?"

"You could run a beauty school. Look at you! You could be a teacher." Anping had anticipated the question. "Or you can work with my grandson. He has his own business."

"But I don't have an Earth hukou."

"My grandson has an Earth hukou. And I will have mine back as soon as I pay off the mortgage. He can sponsor you. He's the last of my husband's surname. It's survival of the family. Under the constitution of Original China, it would be legal for him to sponsor you."

"But what if I don't get better? He wouldn't want a sick wife."

"You'll get better on Earth. It's the radiation on Mars that's making you ill," Anping said quickly. She watched Xiao Ling's face closely, trying to gauge whether she believed. Anping knew that it might not be the radiation. It might be the nature of clones. They didn't live as long as originals. Even she knew this. Maybe this is what the end looked like, and the doctors here had merely told Xiao Ling it was the cancer that affected originals so that she wouldn't get angry, so that she wouldn't make a fuss. But there was a chance Anping's guess about Mars was correct. Who could say really?

Xiao Ling seemed willing to believe Anping. She asked a different question now. "What if Hua Hua's father wants to keep her and won't let her go?"

"How long have I lived with you and he hasn't called once? How long has it been since he last saw you? Normal fathers would be concerned about their child."

Xiao Ling looked as though she might start crying. The tip of her nose turned red and her eyes teared up. Anping could almost believe the clone did feel real emotions, even though this was supposed to be impossible.

"Don't worry. You will become our family. And we will love Hua Hua as our own blood."

Xiao Ling didn't say anything more, but Anping noted that she didn't look as skeptical as she had when Anping first spoke. Even better, she didn't cry.

. . .

After that, every night after Hua Hua went to sleep, Anping talked with Xiao Ling about her plan. She talked about the village. She talked about the families. She talked about the gratitude everyone would feel to have such a teacher in their midst.

"My husband and my grandson will be thrilled when they hear the good news," Anping said.

Xiao Ling began to look more optimistic. After a couple of weeks, she even took up performing along with the soap operas again, even though she had to stop and rest every now and then because of her fatigue. Hua Hua seemed not to notice but followed her mother around the room, imitating her gestures, playing along.

Then one night Anping overheard Xiao Ling talking to Hua Hua as she put the girl to bed. "Would you like to go on a trip sometime? Wouldn't that be fun? We could have a real adventure!"

"Will Ayi come with us?" Hua Hua asked hesitantly.

"Oh yes, she will!" Xiao Ling assured her.

Anping hurried away from their door. She didn't want to be caught eavesdropping and ruin the moment. She hurried to her own room and shut the door, then exhaled. A weight seemed to lift off her chest, a weight she hadn't even realized had been there. Suddenly Anping could imagine a future, a real family, all of them seated around the table in their kitchen. Perhaps Xiao Ling's health might really improve in the village. They could be happy together, three generations living under one roof. It wasn't quite the traditional sort of generations, but if she waited for her grandson to marry and have a child the old-fashioned way, she might be too old to enjoy the child. No, she realized, this really was the ideal solution.

. . .

The next day Anping went for a walk in the courtyard while Hua Hua was at school and Xiao Ling was resting. She didn't want to hover over Xiao Ling and worry her. Xiao Ling needed to keep her spirits up so that she could be strong enough for the journey. The solar flare period would ease soon, and she'd be able to call her grandson back on Earth. She'd tell him her plan without mentioning the complications about Xiao Ling's origins so that he could start the paperwork to sponsor a wife. And of course so that Xiao Ling and her grandson could meet and get to know each other over the satellite phone. Naturally her grandson would be surprised, but she was certain he'd be taken by the beautiful woman. Besides, she was his grandmother, and she knew what was best for him. How could he complain about her impeccable plan?

Anping was rounding the bend by the koi fountain of virtual water, a spring in her step, pleased with her own cleverness, when the man with the dog appeared on the walkway headed toward her.

Such an unpleasant creature. It had reddish eyes and sharp teeth that protruded from its underbite. It took after its owner, who did not smile at Anping but merely scowled at her arrogantly.

Anping tried to smile to ease the tension, but then she got a whiff of the man's breath even from so many feet away. He'd been drinking! Anping stepped away from the man and tried to pass by quickly.

"Whassamatter, Grandma?" the man slurred. He made a lewd gesture then blocked her path.

"You have no face," Anping shot back. "It's not even ten in the morning and you're drunk."

The man swore at her.

"Shut your mouth!" she commanded.

The dog snarled, and before she could jump away, it leaped forward and bit her leg. She could feel its strong teeth in her flesh, a quick nasty bite.

"Aiya!" Anping kicked the dog as hard as she could. Surprisingly, it yelped.

"Hey, that's my dog!" the man said stupidly.

"Watch your dog!"

The dog growled, it lowered its head and circled her.

"Get back!" she said firmly. "I'll kick you again!" Before the dog could attack again, Anping grabbed hold of one of the artificial potted ferns. It was heavy, made of some kind of plaster, and she held it over the dog's head, aiming.

The dog rushed toward her, and she struck it as hard as she could with the planter.

To her surprise, the dog's nose broke off its face, exposing the circuits beneath. It was not a real dog at all, but a cyborg, so realistic she'd never have believed it if she couldn't see its wiring with her own eyes. Confused, the robot dog ceased its snarling and instead ran in a circle, chasing its tail, emitting smoke from its head.

"Ta ma de!" the man shouted. "You bitch! You know how much my dog cost?"

A police drone circled overhead, its lights flashing red and blue.

Someone within the building must have called security. The drone swooped down, its siren wailing.

"Hands up! Don't move!" a mechanical voice commanded. The drone shone a bright beam in Anping's eyes.

"Wait!" said Anping, squinting. "I was the one who was attacked!"

But another police drone arrived and circled round the busted robodog, which had tipped over, its legs running in place as gray smoke billowed from its broken head.

A police pod car arrived, and Anping stood helplessly in place as the police officers jumped out, their weapons pointed at her chest. They placed her in restraints and forced her into their pod car.

Anping was furious that the police were more concerned that she had broken one man's expensive toy than the fact that the malfunctioning toy had bitten her. "Do you know how much a dog like that costs?" the booking officer said. "Ha! You'd have to work for more than ten years just to have one with half of that dog's features!"

She was forced to spend the night in lockup, in suspended animation in one of the coffin-sized cells. While she was sleeping, someone ended up calling the employment agency, and by the time Anping was awakened, Miss Sally was there in the police waiting room, looking expensive in her suit and heels and all her makeup. But at least she bailed Anping out.

She even got them to drop the charges, Sally explained to Anping in the drive back to the apartment complex.

"You're very fortunate that your employer is very sympathetic and he likes the job you've been doing. Some men are very difficult and wouldn't care."

"You mean Xiao Ling. She's my employer."

"No, Xiao Ling is the client for our agency, but she's not technically your employer. You're lucky your employer has just returned from New Taiwan."

Anping was shocked. She'd assumed he would stay out of the picture. "How long is he staying?"

"Not long this time."

"This time? Is he worried about Xiao Ling's health?"

"You could say that," Sally said. "Anyway, it's best not to ask too many questions. You're lucky he was willing to vouch for you with the police. The police are intimidated by money."

That was one way to put it, Anping thought.

. . .

Back at the apartment complex, Anping was surprised to see all the plants in the courtyard had been changed. No longer filled with potted ferns, there were instead planters filled with artificial blooming roses, indicating it was now considered summer in the colony.

"How long was I in that cell?" Anping asked, suddenly worried.

"About three weeks."

"What? I wasn't even charged!"

"It took a while to make the arrangements to bail you out, and then the bribes so they wouldn't charge you." Sally shook her head. "That was a very expensive dog you broke."

They took the elevator to the apartment, and when the door opened, there was a man seated in the main room, lounging on the sofa. At first glance, Anping had no idea who it was, then she realized it must have been the man in the photograph with Xiao Ling and Hua Hua, except that he had aged several decades. Anping wondered how it was possible he had aged so much when Hua Hua was only a year or so older than she'd been in the photo.

"I've brought Ayi back, Mr. Wen," Sally said brightly. "Thank you, thank you. The nanny is very grateful for all your help."

Anping took her cue from Sally's behavior. "I'm very grateful," she said. "This was a terrible misunderstanding."

Sally shot her a look, but before Anping could explain further, the door to Xiao Ling's bedroom opened.

"Ayi, you're back! Did you enjoy your vacation? Hua Hua and I missed you!"

Anping stared at the young woman before her. She resembled Xiao Ling exactly except that she appeared to be at least a dozen years younger. Her face was full, her hair thick, her skin bright, radiating health.

"Where—" Anping began then stopped herself. "Where is Hua Hua?"

"Hua Hua is at school of course."

"Actually Hua Hua is visiting a friend," said the old man.

"Oh. Hua Hua is visiting a friend," the young woman repeated.

Anping swallowed. She looked at the old man, who was smiling, exposing his nicotine-stained teeth. The clone hurried over to the old man and kissed him on top of his head.

"Well, well, well," he said happily.

"I'd better head out. I've got to get back to the office," Sally said. She turned on her heel.

Anping followed her to hallway.

"What has happened?"

"Oh, well, you were bound to find out, and Mr. Wen thought you might as well know the truth. So he decided Xiao Ling should make her transition sooner rather than later."

"What does that mean? What has he done to Xiao Ling?"

"Why, that is Xiao Ling," Sally said. "She has all Xiao Ling's old memories. Or at least most of them. Not the memories of her illness of course. That would be cruel."

"You wanted the police to keep me locked up," Anping said. "That's why you waited three weeks. So they could take her away and bring in this, this, this thing."

"She is the same as Xiao Ling. Genetically identical. Except she isn't sick."

"Not yet."

"Maybe not ever," said Sally. "Each model improves so fast." They were at the elevator. "Look, Anping, this is a good job for you, isn't it? Aren't you paid well? The family likes you. The employer likes you. And that's what's most important. Don't make a fuss." Sally stepped in the elevator and the door closed with a hiss.

. . .

When Anping returned to the apartment, she noticed the photograph of the family had disappeared. The walls were smooth and blank. Xiao Ling had retired to bed early, and Anping found herself alone with Mr. Wen.

He sat at the kitchen table, drinking a hot tea.

"Where is Hua Hua really?"

"Don't worry," he said. "She's very safe. Just getting a memory upgrade."

"She's a clone too?"

"No, of course not. It's illegal to clone children. Besides, there's no way to prevent clones from aging. At some point a clone would grow up. She wouldn't be able to stay sweet and innocent like this."

Anping felt a wave of cold run across her entire body. "She's a cyborg," Anping said, understanding at last. "I didn't realize they could be so realistic."

The old man nodded proudly. "Actually she's my creation. I manufactured her in our company. She's a prototype. Almost perfect."

"Almost?"

"We have a few kinks in the circuits to work out," he said. "That's one reason I've been away so long. Too long."

"Is she going to suffer like her mother? Is she going to get sick?" Despite herself, Anping felt protective of Hua Hua.

"Xiao Ling isn't her bio-mother," the old man said. "And I wouldn't call what they go through suffering. The new model never remembers anyway. I don't implant the bad memories. They always start over with only the happy memories. And little Hua Hua won't remember anything I don't want her to."

Anping felt sick but didn't dare let her disgust show. "What's the problem with Hua Hua then?"

"Too much free will." He sighed. "I wanted a sweet daughter, but this one keeps imitating Xiao Ling."

"That's not a problem. That's natural for a daughter."

"Perhaps," he said. "Perhaps not."

Anping despised him. He was even worse than she had imagined. Not just arrogant, not just someone who used women, but worse. Someone trying to design women and girls to be less than human just to satisfy his ego. "Why are you still getting old?" she asked at last.

"What do you mean?" He frowned, offended.

"You can do all this. Make a daughter who is forever a young child. Implant Xiao Ling's memories into a younger body. Why don't you save yourself?" Anping pointed at his nose. "How long has this been going on? I saw the other picture. You are the only one getting older."

"I'm an original human," he said. "My memories can't be implanted safely into another body. I don't want to lose anything."

"Someone must have been Xiao Ling's original."

"It's not the same," said Mr. Wen, his lips pressed together into a thin flat line. "I have a superior intellect. I shouldn't be imitated. My creative thinking is what drives my inventions. It's what makes my company a success."

What a vain monster, thought Anping. Playing with other people's lives. Despite what he thought of Xiao Ling and Hua Hua, Anping considered them people, just as good as originals. She wasn't even sure what the distinctions were anymore.

"Is it true what you told Xiao Ling about your other family? Do you even have a real wife and family?" Anping asked.

"Oh, yes, that's very true. Although my first wife passed away, bless her, and our children are grown, but I have a second wife. And she's an original of course. And our children are originals."

"Is Xiao Ling your only . . ." Anping wasn't sure what to call her.

"Oh, no, of course not. I can't help it. I love my experiments. I have multiple experiments ongoing in fact," he said, pleased with himself.

Anping had seen men like this all her life. Arrogant wealthy men with better connections, more money, powerful families who thought they were better than everyone else because they were born luckier. But she also knew how to manage such men. She hurried over to the stove and brought the man more hot water for his tea. She brought out some of the snacks in the refrigerator, the colony-grown litchis, a bowl of sliced mangos. They were smaller and harder and drier than Earth mangos, but at least not as tasteless as the colony-grown soy protein supplements. She set the fruit on the table before Mr. Wen.

"Aiya! This world really is amazing!" she said. "I'm from a village, and I couldn't even imagine such things. You must be a genius."

"Yes," said the man. "I am." He picked up a litchi with his short, dry fingers.

"I'm honored to meet you. Thank you for helping me with the police and their mistake. I'll work twice as hard for you now," Anping said. "I'm forever grateful."

"It's the least I could do," he said smugly. "I can tell you're a good nanny. Hua Hua is very fond of you. She was worried about you."

"Such a sweet girl," Anping agreed. "She'll be so happy you're going to be staying with us for a while."

"Oh, unfortunately, I will be leaving again very soon."

"Heavens!" said Anping, secretly delighted. "You've only just arrived! Hua Hua will miss you so much."

The man glowed. "Yes, I'm sure she will. But I have my other experiments to attend to. And I don't want anyone to get spoiled."

"But you'll come back soon?"

"I have work to attend to. In the meantime, Xiao Ling needs time to adjust. It takes a period for her memories to adjust to the new body."

"So complicated," said Anping, making her voice as stupid as possible. "How long does that take?"

"It depends. It could be months. I don't like to deal with the transition period. It can be messy. Emotions pop up on pathways that haven't been completely overridden. There can be crying. I don't like to see this. But my doctors will see to her mood stabilization. Then I'll be back. In fact it might be a year or so."

"Or so? Oh, dear. Poor Hua Hua. She'll miss you. She talks about her father all the time." Anping was surprised she could lie so easily.

"Does she?" the old man smiled, his lips pulling back from his teeth, the skin along his cheeks cracking. "Sweet little thing. But it doesn't matter really. I've got her on meds so she won't grow up. So when I come back again, she'll still be her sweet little self."

"Ah, I see. That's why she has to eat the special food."

"Yes, you understand why it's so important. Nutrients for cyborgs, it's a whole new technology. A little more of this and a little less of that, and you've got a cyborg aging like a human. Can't have that."

"No," said Anping. "That would be terrible."

"Terrible," agreed the old man.

■ ■ ■

That night, the old man slept in Xiao Ling's room, and Anping made sure to keep her door closed so that she would not have to hear them or anything that might make her imagine what went on between them when they were alone together.

Still, she could not sleep. Her mind was racing with plans and possibilities. A year was a useful amount of time. Time to find out what exactly Xiao Ling remembered of their conversations together. Time to find out if Xiao Ling's personality had survived the transition. Time to contact her husband and grandson. Time for paperwork and red tape. Time to pay down her mortgage.

Mr. Wen wanted to believe that Xiao Ling was stupid and would love him forever, but Anping knew Xiao Ling had been willing to listen to Anping's exit plan.

Anping lay back in her bed, pleased with her plotting. The rich man shouldn't have kept making his cloned lover younger; he should have tried to make his own body less old. Soon he'd be too old to be a problem.

Back in her village, before she'd left Earth, Anping had always blamed young women for getting involved with such men, willing to play the concubine, chasing after money for temporary ease, but she had not thought really about the selfishness of wealthy men. Their selfishness had seemed natural and unavoidable, but now she also saw the arrogance that could make such a man blind.

Mr. Wen might have been a genius, but he was also certainly a fool.

After the old man left, Anping was confident that she'd find a way to bring Xiao Ling and Hua Hua back to her village. A family was a precious thing, not to be wasted. Anping would not abandon hers, neither the one on Earth, nor this new one she'd found. None of them was perfect by traditional standards, it was true, but together they made a pretty good family for this strange, new time they were living in.

ACKNOWLEDGMENTS

Special thanks to the following editors and journals who first published stories from this collection in somewhat different form: Evelyn Somers-Rogers and Speer Morgan, *Missouri Review*; Beth Staples, *Shenandoah*; Joseph Lease, *Eleven Eleven*; and Polly Rosenwaike, Khaled Mattawa, and Aaron Stone, *Michigan Quarterly Review*.

Thank you to my colleagues and students at San Francisco State University, who continue to inspire me; Dean Andrew Harris; and to the College of Liberal and Creative Arts, whose Research, Scholarly, and Creative Activity (RSCA) Grant for work delayed because of the COVID-19 pandemic enabled me to complete this book.

Many thanks to my friends and family for all their support during the writing of these stories, especially during these stressful times of rising anti-Asian violence and attacks and the terrors of the pandemic: Lenore Chinn, Nina de Gramont, Hannah dela Cruz Abrams, Carolyn Desalu, Gwynn Gacosta, Bob Hsiang, Nancy Hom, Gary Kramer, Lucien Kubo, Scott Lankford, Serena Lee, Felicia Luna Lemus, George Lew, Melody Moezzi, Bleriana Myftiu, Edith Oxfeld, Ellen Oxfeld, Lorraine Saulino-Klein, Cindy Shih, Leon Sun, Nara Takakawa, Frances Kai-Hwa Wang, Nina Wolff, Tamiko Wong, Susan Xin Xu, and Xiaojie Zheng. Thank you to Clare Beams, K-Ming Chang, Margaret Wilkerson Sexton, and Charles Yu for your support. Very special thanks to the light of my life, Ariel Chai Horn, and my father, Winberg Chai, for his love and faith.

Finally, I am deeply grateful to Team Blair for taking such good care of this manuscript, including cover designer Laura Williams; the resourceful Kelsie Roper; my superbly talented, patient, and sharp-eyed editor, Robin Miura; and my ingenious publisher, Lynn York.